AVAILABLE NOW!

LEARNING TO RIDE

City girl Madeline Harper never wanted to love a cowboy. But rodeo king Tanner Callen might change her mind…and win her heart.

THE McCULLAGH INN IN MAINE

Chelsea O'Kane escapes to Maine to build a new life—until she runs into Jeremy Holland, an old flame.…

SACKING THE QUARTERBACK

Attorney Melissa St. James wins every case. Now, when she's up against football superstar Grayson Knight, her heart is on the line, too.

THE MATING SEASON

Documentary ornithologist Sophie Castle is convinced that her heart belongs only to the birds—until she meets her gorgeous cameraman, Rigg Greensman.

THE RETURN

Ashley Montoya was in love with Mack McLeroy in high school—until he broke her heart. But when an accident brings him back to Sunnybell to recover, Ashley can't help but fall into his embrace.…

DAZZLING: THE DIAMOND TRILOGY, BOOK I

To support her artistic career, Siobhan Dempsey works at the elite Stone Room in New York City...never expecting to be swept away by Derick Miller.

BODYGUARD

Special Agent Abbie Whitmore has only one task: protect Congressman Jonathan Lassiter from a violent cartel's threats. Yet she's never had to do it while falling in love....

BOOK**SHOTS**

CROSS KILL

Along Came a Spider killer Gary Soneji died years ago. But Alex Cross swears he sees Soneji gun down his partner. Is his greatest enemy back from the grave?

ZOO 2

Humans are evolving into a savage new species that could save civilization—or end it. James Patterson's *Zoo* was just the beginning.

THE TRIAL

An accused killer will do anything to disrupt his own trial, including a courtroom shocker that Lindsay Boxer and the Women's Murder Club will never see coming.

LITTLE BLACK DRESS

Can a little black dress change everything? What begins as one woman's fantasy is about to go too far.

LET'S PLAY MAKE-BELIEVE

Christy and Marty just met, and it's love at first sight. Or is it? One of them is playing a dangerous game—and only one will survive.

CHASE

A man falls to his death in an apparent accident....But why does he have the fingerprints of another man who is already dead? Detective Michael Bennett is on the case.

HUNTED

Someone is luring men from the streets to play a mysterious, high-stakes game. Former Special Forces officer David Shelley goes undercover to shut it down—but will he win?

113 MINUTES

Molly Rourke's son has been murdered. Now she'll do whatever it takes to get justice. No one should underestimate a mother's love....

$10,000,000 MARRIAGE PROPOSAL

A mysterious billboard offering $10 million to get married intrigues three single women in LA. But who is Mr. Right...and is he the perfect match for the lucky winner?

FRENCH KISS

It's hard enough to move to a new city, but now everyone French detective Luc Moncrief cares about is being killed off. Welcome to New York.

KILLER CHEF

Caleb Rooney knows how to do two things: run a food truck and solve a murder. When people suddenly start dying of food-borne illnesses, the stakes are higher than ever....

UPCOMING ROMANCES

RADIANT: THE DIAMOND TRILOGY, BOOK II

After an explosive breakup with her billionaire boyfriend, Siobhan Dempsey moves to Detroit to pursue her art. But Derick isn't ready to give her up.

HOT WINTER NIGHTS

Allie Thatcher moved to Montana to start fresh as the head of the trauma center. And even though the days are cold, the nights are steamy…especially when she meets search-and-rescue leader Dex Belmont.

UPCOMING THRILLERS
BOOK**SHOTS**

THE CHRISTMAS MYSTERY

Two stolen paintings disappear from a Park Avenue murder scene— French detective Luc Moncrief is in for a merry Christmas.

COME AND GET US

When an SUV deliberately runs Miranda Cooper and her husband off a desolate Arizona road, she must run for help alone as his cryptic parting words echo in her head: "Be careful who you trust."

PRIVATE: THE ROYALS

After kidnappers threaten to execute a Royal Family member in front of the Queen, Jack Morgan and his elite team of PIs have just twenty-four hours to stop them. Or heads will roll…literally.

BLACK & BLUE

Detective Harry Blue is determined to take down the serial killer who's abducted several women, but her mission leads to a shocking revelation.

THE MOST ELIGIBLE BACHELOR ON CAPITOL HILL HAS MET HIS MATCH.

Abbie Whitmore is good at her security job—until Congressman Jonathan Lassiter comes along. The presidential hopeful refuses to believe that he's in danger, even though Abbie's determined to keep him safe. But how can she protect him while she's guarding her own heart?

BODYGUARD

BY JESSICA LINDEN

**READ THE SUSPENSEFUL ROMANCE,
AVAILABLE NOW FROM**

Dazzling

The Diamond Trilogy:
Book 1

ELIZABETH HAYLEY

FOREWORD BY

JAMES PATTERSON

Little, Brown and Company

New York Boston London

Copyright © 2016 by James Patterson

Hachette Book Group supports the right to free expression and the value of copyright. The purpose of copyright is to encourage writers and artists to produce the creative works that enrich our culture.

The scanning, uploading, and distribution of this book without permission is a theft of the author's intellectual property. If you would like permission to use material from the book (other than for review purposes), please contact permissions@hbgusa.com. Thank you for your support of the author's rights.

BookShots / Little, Brown and Company
Hachette Book Group
1290 Avenue of the Americas, New York, NY 10104
bookshots.com

First Edition: November 2016

BookShots is an imprint of Little, Brown and Company, a division of Hachette Book Group, Inc. The Little, Brown name and logo are trademarks of Hachette Book Group, Inc. The BookShots name and logo are trademarks of JBP Business, LLC.

The publisher is not responsible for websites (or their content) that are not owned by the publisher.

The Hachette Speakers Bureau provides a wide range of authors for speaking events. To find out more, go to hachettespeakersbureau.com or call (866) 376-6591.

ISBN 978-0-316-27643-6
LCCN 2016938291

10 9 8 7 6 5 4 3 2 1

LSC-C

Printed in the United States of America

FOREWORD

When I first had the idea for BookShots, I knew that I wanted to include romantic stories. The whole point of BookShots is to give people lightning-fast reads that completely capture them for just a couple of hours in their day—so publishing romance felt right.

I have a lot of respect for romance authors. I took a stab at the genre when I wrote *Suzanne's Diary for Nicholas* and *Sundays at Tiffany's*. While I was happy with the results, I learned that the process of writing those stories required hard work and dedication.

That's why I wanted to pair up with the best romance authors for BookShots. I work with writers who know how to draw emotions out of their characters, all while catapulting their plots forward.

Author team Elizabeth Hayley is one of those dynamite writing forces in romance. In this story, *Dazzling,* you're getting the first book in a gut-wrenching, dramatic serial romance. Only a team like this could write the passion you'll find here. And while *Dazzling* ends on a cliffhanger, I know that next month, you'll be back for more.

James Patterson

Dazzling

Chapter 1

"AND REMEMBER TO tell people about the step down into the lounge."

Siobhan Dempsey tried to hide her boredom. She knew she should pay attention to Saul's words as he droned on and on about how he wanted his lounge run. But honestly, a girl could only have a balding, sixty-something-year-old man tell her that "flirting paid the bills" so many times.

She got it. All the servers and bartenders at the Stone Room did. The place was aptly named, not just because of the stunning exposed stone walls, but also because of the various gems that adorned everything from the diamond chandeliers to the ruby napkin holders.

Wealthy men flocked to this high-end bar from all over the country. Not only was it housed in one of the ritziest hotels in New York, but its beautiful employees were classy enough to keep their clothes on, yet risqué enough to show a little skin. The uniform at the Stone Room could best be described as expensively sexy in all black.

"Elegant black," as Saul called it. The kind that required silk and stilettos. How low the neckline dipped and how high the hem rose resulted in how much cash a girl wanted to leave with at the end of the night. Needless to say, none of the girls ever complained about the money.

Letting her eyes drift over the plush slate-gray couches that sat atop dark hardwood floors, Siobhan was still surprised that she worked here. Before moving to New York, she'd only ever seen places like the Stone Room in movies. They certainly didn't exist in Oklahoma.

She glanced past the sleek mahogany bar to the mirror behind the liquor shelves, checking her reflection before the place opened. She ran her fingers through her long, light-brown hair, which appeared significantly darker in the dim lighting, and practiced her "happy to be seating you" smile.

The Stone Room screamed opulence and glamour. Siobhan had never felt so out of place in her life. She had no clue why Saul had given her the job three months ago, but she knew better than to question him. The money was good, and she didn't have to do anything that would potentially get her arrested.

She looked at the other workers, whose ability to feign interest came naturally. Most of the bartenders and servers were performing artists. Siobhan guessed Saul thought they'd be able to put on a show for the customers, which explained why she was relegated to hosting duties. Evidently painters, like their art, were better observed while still. Dropping a tray of crystal stemware during training had probably also made

Saul's decision an easy one. A hostess she was, and a hostess she would likely stay.

That is, if he allowed her to stay at all. Saul had made it clear that one more screw-up would cost her the job. She'd need to curb her innate clumsiness if she was going to keep the job she desperately needed.

The meeting finally ended with a "don't forget to smile seductively" from Saul. Barely managing to suppress a groan, Siobhan stood and turned to Marnel, one of the servers. "Who should I introduce you as tonight?"

Marnel pursed her lips and cast her pale-green eyes to the ceiling, which Siobhan knew was all for show. Marnel never left her apartment without that night's persona firmly in place. She also didn't leave without every blond curl on her head in place. "How about Scarlett?"

Marnel was an aspiring actress who had very peculiar beliefs about fame. The oddest was that her stage name was as important to hitting the big time as her talent was. So she picked a new one each shift with the hopes that it would click and she'd instantly be catapulted to stardom. Or something like that.

Siobhan shrugged. "I don't know why you don't just use your own name. It's so unique."

"I've been Marnel for twenty-six years, and the only thing it ever got me was the nickname Nell and questions about growing up in the forest."

Siobhan squinted. "I'm guessing that I'm supposed to know what that means."

It looked like Marnel was about to launch off on her when Cory appeared holding a serving tray. "What what means?"

Pointing a finger at Siobhan, Marnel answered. "She's never seen the movie *Nell*."

Cory tilted her head slightly. "Okay, not quite the conversation I'd anticipated."

"What were you anticipating?" Siobhan asked.

"Pretty much anything besides that."

The girls' laughter was interrupted by a stern-looking Saul. "I've opened the doors. Try to act professional," he said, before walking off.

"Lucky for him, I can act like I'm anything. Including a southern belle named Scarlett," Marnel said, with an over-emphasized twang.

Siobhan cocked an eyebrow playfully. "I've never met a southern belle in a black lace bustier and leather shorts."

Marnel smirked as she backed away from them. "Then you ain't met the right kind, darlin'."

Siobhan shook her head as a grin spread across her face.

"She's something else," Cory said. "I better get to my station. Remember to seat all the handsome guys with me." She shot Siobhan a wink before retreating to her side of the lounge.

Letting her eyes drift over the large room one more time, Siobhan made her way toward the front of the house. She tried not to limp as she walked. She never usually wore heels, and she wondered how long she'd have to shove her feet into five-inch stilettos before her art could pay the bills. It wasn't that she hated her job. The girls were fun, and the patrons were mostly nice. But she was an artist, not a model. Her feet could only withstand so much mistreatment.

Suddenly, Siobhan tripped and it was too late to catch herself. It was one of those slow-motion moments where the floor inches toward a person's face. Siobhan felt like every person in that room was not only incredibly attractive, but had their eyes glued to her, that chick in the black minidress and peep-toe pumps who was about to eat the hardwood.

As Siobhan braced for the moment of impact, all she could think about was how this was yet another reminder that she didn't belong here and would likely not be allowed to stay. Nothing said fluid sex kitten like plunging to the floor, landing on all fours, and clawing at your fleeing dignity.

But just before she made contact with the ground, a strong hand gripped her biceps from behind and kept her on her feet. As the gentleman helped right her, she turned toward him, though she wasn't quite ready to lift her head yet.

Realizing that she couldn't stare at the floor all night, her blue eyes began their slow ascent up the man in the navy-blue trousers. She started her apology somewhere around his belt. "I'm so sorry." She took in his pressed-to-perfection white button-down. "Thank you." No tie, but a collar that had one button open to show off a hint of tanned skin. "Seriously, thank you…" Then her eyes locked with his. *Sweet Mother of God.*

Chapter 2

SIOBHAN HAD TO remind herself to breathe. And to listen, because the gorgeous man in front of her was talking. *Wait…oh shit, he's talking to me.* "I'm sorry. What was that?"

His answering smile showed perfect teeth that looked immaculately white against the darkness of his trimmed beard. Light-brown eyes crinkled with humor. This was a man who obviously laughed a lot. "I asked if you were all right."

Suddenly aware that she was still gripping onto the forearm she must've grabbed when he'd caught her, she snatched her hand back as she straightened up fully, nearly causing her to lose her balance a second time. "Yeah. I mean yes. Yes, I'm okay. Thank you."

Leaning back slightly, he pushed his hands into his pockets. *God, he's tall.* Siobhan was five feet seven inches without the torturous heels. The man in front of her had to be quite a few inches over six feet. "You're welcome."

He stood in front of her, staring with a small smirk on his lips. *His lips.* They were full without being too plump. Siobhan thought about how soft they'd probably feel against her own mouth. How the coarse scruff on his face would offset the smoothness of his lips, creating a delicious friction that would keep her locked in the moment.

That strong hand that had gripped her arm would slide around her back and pull her into him where she'd get to revel in the hardness of what was surely a strong, lean body. Not that she knew he was well-built for sure, but that's what daydreaming was for. *Daydreaming? Oh my God, I'm doing it again.*

Siobhan gave herself a mental shake. "Sorry."

"Do you always do that?"

"Do what?" She quickly looked down at herself to see if he could possibly be talking about some other embarrassing thing she was doing instead of calling her out on her obvious lack of grace.

"Apologize."

She narrowed her eyes in confusion. "Sorry?"

He laughed. "You did it again."

Why was she acting like such a moron? She was twenty-seven years old, not fourteen. "I meant that *sorry* as an *excuse me*."

"Did you do something inappropriate?"

"What?" she asked before she could remind herself to be polite.

"Did you do something I need to excuse you for?"

Why was this guy messing with her? Why couldn't he be like most New Yorkers and ignore her existence? "You mean other than forcing you to keep me from smashing my face into the floor?"

He rocked back and forth on his heels before answering. "How exactly did you *force* me to do that?"

"Well, I guess I didn't literally force you. Most guys probably would've done what you did."

His smile dropped as his brows furrowed. "I'm not sure I like being compared to most guys."

"You'd prefer me to compare you to the few assholes who'd have let me fall?" Siobhan mentally slapped herself. Granted, she hadn't paid much attention during Saul's meeting, but she was fairly certain using profanity in front of customers had been covered. And if not, it should have been.

Her dream man barked out a laugh before extending his hand toward her. "I'm Derick."

She put her hand into his. "Siobhan."

"Siobhan. That's a beautiful name." He stopped shaking her hand, but didn't release it.

"Thank you," she replied, her voice barely above a whisper.

He stepped closer. "You've done that a lot, too."

Siobhan looked up at him, mesmerized by his amber eyes. "Done what?"

"Thanked me."

"I have a lot to thank you for."

Derick opened his mouth to say something else, but was cut off by Saul's gruff voice. "Siobhan, you're needed at the front desk."

She quickly retracted her hand and looked over at her boss who had stopped beside her. "Right. On my way." She glanced at Derick as she passed. "Thanks again."

Hurrying to the hostess stand, she immersed herself in catching up on seating guests and answering phones with her coworker Tiffany.

"Siobhan, the girls are falling behind. You think you can help run drinks for a few minutes without screwing anything up?" Saul asked. "Tiffany can cover the front for a bit."

"Sure." *I hope.* Saul must have been really desperate to ask her. He'd made it clear that she was on thin ice. Asking her to carry liquid in fine glassware to paying customers seemed like a set-up. She briskly made her way to the servers' station at the corner of the bar. "Hey, Blaine."

Blaine tucked a piece of her black hair behind her ear as she strained a martini into a glass. "Hey." She smiled. "What are you doing over here?"

"Saul asked me to help run drinks."

Blaine mashed her lips together as though she were stifling a laugh. "Maybe you shouldn't *run* with them."

"Ha-ha, very funny. So I guess you saw my little incident earlier."

Blaine's blue eyes sparkled with amusement. "I did."

Siobhan began lining up the drinks on a tray so that she could carry it steadily, when a voice caused her to jolt and spill liquor all over her hand.

"I figured out how you can thank me."

Siobhan whipped her head around as she reached for a bar napkin. *Derick.* "How's that?" she asked, wondering if Derick recognized the wariness in her voice. Her knight in shining armor was quickly devolving into a sleazy frat boy. Her mind ran through a list of possible ways he would make her repay the debt.

"Go to lunch with me tomorrow."

That had definitely not made her list. "Lunch?"

He leaned against the bar. "Yeah. I have to be in New Jersey for dinner, but I'd like to meet you for lunch before I have to leave the city."

"Sorry. I can't."

"Why not?"

Because I turn into a bumbling idiot whenever you're around. "I just can't."

"I don't accept that as a valid excuse."

"Why should it matter to me whether or not you think my excuse is valid?"

He thought for a second. "Because I'm handsome?"

Siobhan couldn't help the laugh that tumbled out of her. "I'm not making an excuse. I really can't. I teach an art class in Central Park on Sundays."

"Oh. Well, that is a pretty good excuse. Sounds like a lot of fun."

She nodded.

"Okay. I guess I'll see you then." Derick turned and walked away.

Siobhan stood still for a few moments, too shocked to move. How could someone who had seemed so adamant about meeting her for lunch give up so easily? She had to admit, it was a little disappointing. Because not only had he walked away—but he'd also looked damned happy to do so.

Chapter 3

AS DERICK FUMBLED with the iced coffees and plastic bag of supplies he'd been carrying, he began to hate Central Park. He had no idea where the hell he was actually headed. He'd already walked almost two miles and was quickly running out of places to check. He looked out onto the expansive lawn. Even with trees on either side of him, the summer sun caused him to squint. *If I were an art class, where would I be?*

Unfortunately, he had no answer for the voice that had been plaguing him since he'd entered the park. Derick glanced at his watch, nearly spilling coffee on himself as he turned his wrist to check the time. *Shit.*

It was almost one, and the bartender at the Stone Room had told him the class began at twelve thirty. If Siobhan hadn't left for the night by the time he'd thought to ask, he could have gotten the exact location, too. At this rate, when he finally got to wherever the class was, it would be over. He looked for a trash can to toss the coffees, which were getting warm. But then he saw her.

She was about thirty feet away, her long hair pulled up loosely in one of those hairstyles that only hot chicks can make sexy. He remembered Siobhan's hair being a medium brown. But now, in the midday sun, he could make out hints of copper in it. He'd loved the way it looked last night, with long, natural waves resting about halfway down her back. But after seeing the exposed skin on Siobhan's shoulder where the neck of her oversized T-shirt slid down almost to her bicep, this hairstyle was a close second.

Instantly, a satisfied smile came over him as he made his way toward her. She hadn't noticed him yet as the brush in her hand moved delicately over the canvas in front of her. Derick didn't take his eyes off her as he approached. He would have forgotten she was teaching a class if it weren't for the sound of Siobhan's instructions.

"Don't focus too much on shape. Just let your brush find its place on the canvas."

"I'm not too late, am I?" Derick asked, when he finally made it across the lawn to the front of the class.

Siobhan nearly jumped at the sound of his voice, causing some of the paint on the tray of watercolors she'd been holding to splash. But she quickly righted herself—this time without any help. "Derick?"

Confusion swept over her face, though Derick wasn't sure why. When she told him about the art class, he'd said he'd see her then.

"What are you doing here?"

"Same thing everyone else is. Learning to paint," he said, holding up the brown bag that was filled with the art supplies he'd picked up on the way. "I have those. Watercolors, I mean. I didn't know what you'd be using, so I got a little bit of everything to be prepared."

Siobhan's eyes widened and she lowered her voice. "You came to take the class?"

"If I'm being honest, I came to see *you*. But I feel like it might be weird to sit here and stare at you if I'm not painting anything."

A smile ghosted her lips—lips he'd like to taste. And her clear blue eyes twinkled with amusement.

"Oh, and this coffee's for you, if you want it." He extended one cup out to her to take.

"Thanks, that's sweet of you. But I'm more of a tea girl."

Derick laughed softly. "That's good, actually, because I'm pretty sure all the ice melted." Finally he turned toward the class, which he'd just noticed was a sea of elderly women staring at the two of them with rapt attention.

"There's a seat here, honey," a little old woman said, gesturing to the white chair next to her. Derick gave her a grateful smile as he made his way over to sit down. The woman beamed at him. "You smell nice."

Derick didn't quite know what to say, but luckily he'd filtered the *you too* that had nearly rolled off his tongue. Instead, he just took out his large pad of paper and watercolors. He quickly squeezed some onto the small palette and, dipping his brush in the paint, did his best to catch up. Most of the class already had the background painted, so he slapped on some blue to cover the top half of his paper.

It didn't exactly resemble the sky in the other students' work—which was a subtle mixture of crimsons and oranges— but it would have to do. His eyes roamed over the landscape—lush trees, bright-green grass leading down to the pond.

Derick could see why Siobhan had picked this location for her class. But despite its beauty, the park had nothing on Siobhan. The way her worn jeans hugged her ass as she moved the brush across the canvas made him glad he was sitting down. He was definitely hot for Teacher.

But Siobhan's physical attributes weren't the only things that held his attention. The way she proceeded through the class, giving each student a bit of individualized attention as they worked, made her even more alluring. He could tell from the way her face lit up during every interaction that she loved what she did.

Finally, she made her way over to him. "Not bad," she said with a small smile.

He looked at the picture in front of him, which his four-year-old nephew could have painted, and was sure Siobhan was being polite. That or she needed her eyes checked. "Thanks. You're a good teacher. Art isn't really my thing, though."

Siobhan looked intrigued. "No? What *is* your thing?"

As she leaned down a bit, Derick noticed the hint of

bronze shimmering on her cheekbones—a sharp contrast to the dramatic makeup she'd worn last night at the bar. She was even more beautiful without all the cosmetic help. "Since last night?" he said. "You."

Immediately Derick could see the embarrassment redden her face. Though he didn't regret his comment, he felt the need to change the subject so Siobhan would feel more comfortable. "I didn't know how difficult it was to paint with real watercolors. I've only ever used the ones in the white plastic container that kids use. The guy at the art store had to tell me which kind I should get."

Siobhan glanced down into the bag he'd brought with him, which was filled with pastels, oil paints, and charcoal pencils. "Oh my God. You got *all* of that? It probably cost hundreds of dollars."

Derick shrugged. "You said you couldn't do lunch."

"You're a sweet boy." The voice came from the woman next to him. "My husband, God rest his soul, could have learned a thing or two about romance from you. You did all this just so you could see your girlfriend?"

Siobhan's eyes widened. "Oh, we're not…" She gestured between them, shaking her head. "He's not my boyfriend."

Derick glanced up at Siobhan, who couldn't have looked more awkward. Strangely enough, it suited her. "Yeah," he agreed. "She's not my girlfriend." He felt his eyes crinkling with the smile he couldn't hold back. Not that he was trying to. "At least, not yet."

The woman raised her eyes at Siobhan. "Well, what are you waiting for, dear?"

Siobhan glanced at Derick, a twinkle in her eyes that made him hopeful. "We haven't even been out together yet. Crashing my art class doesn't count as a proper date."

Derick chuckled as he finished cleaning up his supplies. "I guess it doesn't." He dropped his things into his bag and stood. "Do you need help getting anything to your car?"

Her eyes narrowed, and she tilted her head slightly. "No, that's okay. I got it."

Derick nodded and shot her a smile, unsure of what could be causing her confusion. Maybe he was reading her wrong. "All right. I'll see you later then." He gave a small wave to the other students who still remained and strode off.

Chapter 4

"WHAT DO YOU mean, he left?" Blaine asked as she put away the glassware in preparation for opening.

Siobhan sighed. "Just what I said. I thought I was making it clear that I wanted him to ask me out, but all he did was offer to help carry my stuff to my car. It was mortifying."

"Do you even have a car?" Blaine asked.

"Is that really the most important detail out of everything I said?"

Blaine shrugged.

"And of course I don't have a car. This is New York."

"I saw him in here a few times since. So he's not avoiding you," Blaine added.

"So I'm the only one who feels awkward. Spectacular." Siobhan's lips pressed into a thin line.

"Well, at least he seems clueless. I'm sure he didn't notice you throwing yourself at him," Marnel chimed in.

"Thanks for that," Siobhan deadpanned. Though she silently hoped Marnel's comment was true. She definitely wanted Derick with a primal urge she hadn't felt before. But she didn't want it to be obvious to *him*. It would be mortifying. She slid her palms over the smoothness of the sleek bar, the subconscious action soothing her frayed nerves.

Until Blaine slapped her fingers. "Stop feeling up my bar. It's not the kind of wood you're after."

Siobhan snatched her hands back. "You girls are supposed to be supportive."

Marnel raised her hands, adopting a meditative stance as she closed her eyes and shook her head, making her blond hair sway behind her. "Oh, I didn't realize. I can work with that. Let me have another shot." When she looked back at Siobhan, her eyes were intense. "It'll all be okay, Siobhan." She placed a hand on Siobhan's shoulder. "One day your prince will come. If you wish upon a star, it makes no difference who—"

Knocking her hand off, Siobhan glared. "You are not seriously quoting a Disney song to me right now. You two totally suck at this."

"Sorry. I wasn't in the right headspace. No Disney. Got it." Marnel stepped toward Siobhan and then grabbed her shoulders before pulling her into a firm hug. "Don't worry, honey. He'll come around and see that you're just a girl, standing in front of a boy, asking him to love her."

Siobhan jerked away. "*Notting Hill*? Really, Marnel?"

Marnel let her arms flare out to her sides before letting them slap back against her thighs. "So *that* you've seen. A *Nell* reference flies right over your head, but you're fluent in *Notting* frigging *Hill?*"

"It's a good movie. And I like Julia Roberts," Siobhan defended, though she quickly realized she had no reason to do so.

But before she could call Marnel out for changing the subject, Marnel started ranting. "Of course you like Julia Roberts. *Everyone* likes Julia Roberts. Whether she's a prostitute or a spoiled diabetic, people rave about her. That's it! I'd planned to be Yvette, but tonight I shall be Julia." She slammed her hand down on the bar for emphasis.

"Better settle down there, Julia. Saul's staring at us," Blaine muttered.

Siobhan snuck a furtive glance. *Definitely staring.* "Okay, I guess I better get to work. Thanks, girls. You were of absolutely no help."

She started to walk away when Blaine's voice stopped her. "For what it's worth, I think this is all just a big misunderstanding. A guy doesn't hunt you down in Central Park just for kicks. So unless he decided to give it a go with one of the Golden Girls, there's a pretty good chance he's interested in you. But you need to relax, or you're going to develop stress-pattern baldness."

Siobhan took a deep breath and digested Blaine's words. "You're right. I need to clear my mind and not obsess over it anymore."

"Thatta girl. Now go introduce Julia to the adoring public."

Siobhan laughed and made her way to the front of the house. She could do this. She could forget about Derick and focus on her job.

And she did. For about ten minutes. Then she started picturing him naked again and got completely sidetracked. She didn't know what her problem was. It wasn't like her to be this flustered by a guy. Siobhan was hardworking and driven—not an obsessive chick who let a simple crush reduce her to a vapid buffoon.

The fact that Derick was having this effect on her was ticking her off. She'd been messing up all night. If she accidentally called Marnel by her real name when introducing her to guests one more time, Marnel might hurt her. Supposedly she was really feeling the Julia mojo, and Siobhan was ruining her chance at fame and fortune.

Siobhan was also ruining her own chances of staying employed at the Stone Room. She'd led guests to an already occupied table twice, knocked over a vase full of flowers and water with a menu, and pulled out a patron's chair without warning him that she'd done so. Thank God the guy had incredible balance and a strong core or he would've been assed out on the floor and Siobhan would've been in deep shit. Thankfully Saul had been taking inventory for most of the night and had missed her trainwreck of an evening.

It got so bad that she barely even registered Derick walking toward her. *Wait…Derick?* "Derick?"

"Hey, Siobhan," he said, as he leaned in for a hug.

Her body returned the hug as her mind scrambled to catch up. Once it did, she dropped her arms.

Derick seemed to sense the shift, because he backed away from her with furrowed brows.

Siobhan's mind was in a state of flux. She was both happy to see him and annoyed as hell.

Shoving his hands in his pockets, he rocked on his heels slightly and smiled at her.

The smile did it. How dare he seem so happy when she'd been going crazy for the past three days? Uh-uh. No way. Smiling was unacceptable. "Party of one, sir?"

Derick raised an eyebrow. "Sir?"

Chapter 5

AS HE WAITED for Siobhan to speak again, Derick did his best to read the woman standing before him. She seemed different than the person he'd met not even a week earlier. And he couldn't figure out why. Four days ago at the park she'd seemed interested in him. At least he thought so.

"'Sir' is how the owner insists we greet customers."

"Okay." Derick smiled, but it felt uneasy. "I guess I thought we were past the formal greetings."

Siobhan grabbed one of the black leather menus from the shelf behind the hostess stand and turned away from him. "Right this way."

Derick followed her as she led him toward the back of the bar to a small table against the wall. He didn't speak again until she'd stopped walking. Then he moved in front of her to look her in the eye, their bodies only inches apart.

He could smell faint traces of her shampoo, but he couldn't quite identify the scent. Almond maybe. "I had hoped that we were moving beyond the hostess-customer relationship. Did I misread that?"

Siobhan closed her eyes for a moment too long to be considered a blink. When she opened them, she cast them toward the floor before bringing back up to meet Derick's. It was one of those gestures people do when they know it's rude to roll their eyes, but they want to get across their annoyance anyway. "I can't…" She released a long sigh that sounded a lot like defeat. "Enjoy your evening." She placed the menu on the dark wood table and turned to leave.

"Siobhan," Derick said after she'd walked a few feet away. "What's going on?"

She stopped but didn't turn around.

"I've been hoping to catch you when you're working. And now that you're finally here, you don't seem like you want to talk to me."

She turned around to face him again. "I guess I could say the same for you."

Derick didn't think it was possible to be more confused than he already was. "What?"

Siobhan crossed her arms over her chest and shot him a look that told him she thought he was an idiot. He didn't disagree. "The art class, Derick. You show up out of the blue talking about how you want to see me. Then when you have an opportunity to ask me out, all you say is, 'Do you need any help getting anything to your car?'"

Well, shit. "I thought I was being nice."

"Look. I'm interested in you. Or I *was*." Siobhan shook her head. "I don't actually know which one." He could hear the uncertainty in her voice, but when she spoke again, she seemed surer of herself. "But what I do know is that I don't need the games. Your server will be right with you."

He could tell she was about to turn around again. But this time he wouldn't let her. At least if he could help it. "I don't want another server. I want *you*."

Siobhan's shoulders seemed to let go of some of the tension they'd been holding, and her eyes softened a bit. "I'm not a server."

Derick stepped a few feet closer to her, closing the small gap between them. "I guess that's true. But that doesn't change my last comment. I want you."

This time Siobhan didn't suppress her eye roll. But some of the anger that had been present a few minutes ago seemed to have dissipated.

Derick took a deep breath as he noticed the light dusting of freckles below her collarbone. God, he'd like to run his tongue over them. "You're beautiful. And the other day at the park," he began, "I wanted to ask you out, but there were elderly women surrounding us, and I was covered in paint and sweat."

"I was covered in paint and sweat, too."

He lifted his hand, letting his fingers tuck Siobhan's wavy hair behind her ear. His thumb toyed with her silver earring that dangled down just low enough to graze her neck as she tilted her head to the side, seemingly waiting for him to respond. He couldn't resist pushing her against the deep crimson wall behind her, causing her breath to hitch. "Yeah," he said softly, "but you looked fucking perfect."

She inhaled deeply and licked her lips. Which was distracting as hell.

"I couldn't ask you out there, like that. It's not really my style," he continued.

"And what *is* your style?" Her voice was hushed, her deep blue eyes twinkling in the dim recessed lighting overhead.

Derick laughed softly. "Apparently it's showing up to a bar four nights straight and making the servers at the Stone Room think I'm an alcoholic."

"I'm sure they don't think that."

Derick paused for a moment. "I actually don't care *what* they think. Because they're not you." He could feel the friction between them evaporate into a sexual thrumming. "So what do you say?" Derick dropped his hands to hers, grasping her fingers between his. "Go out with me tomorrow. Let me take you on a real date—one that doesn't involve paint, watered-down coffee, and other women."

The corners of Siobhan's mouth turned up into a carefree, amused smile.

"Is that a yes?"

"How could I possibly turn down a date that doesn't involve other women?"

He gave her a small smile of relief and lifted a hand to her cheek, gently caressing her skin with his thumb. Almost involuntarily, his face seemed to move closer to hers as if her soft pink lips were drawing him in.

But right as Siobhan's eyes drifted closed, a voice made them both break away. "There you are," Cory said, seeming slightly uncomfortable about interrupting them. "Saul's been looking for you. He's about to flip out."

"Shit," Siobhan whispered as she ran a hand down her clothing.

Cory headed back in the direction she'd come, leaving the two of them alone again.

"You better get back out there," Derick said. "I wouldn't want you to get in trouble. I'll find you before I leave so I can get your number."

Siobhan nodded. "Sounds good. That'll give me time to decide if I want to give it to you."

He could tell she was trying like hell not to crack a smile. And as he watched the way her ass moved in that tight black skirt as she walked away, he hoped that eventually her number wouldn't be all that she'd be giving him.

Chapter 6

SIOBHAN LET HER eyes drift closed as she took another bite of her lobster fra diavolo. "This is seriously amazing," she said, looking across the small table at Derick, who seemed pleased with himself.

"I told you." He held up the bottle of wine he'd brought with them for dinner at the Italian cafe he'd suggested. "More?" he asked.

"Sure. Just a little." She passed him her glass and then helped herself to some more salad from the large bowl that the waiter had placed next to their table.

She took a long drink of her wine to wash down the salad. Noting the label, she identified it as one of the wines the Stone Room carried. And though she had no idea how much it cost, she knew it had to be expensive if the elite bar sold it.

The waiter came back to check on them. "Is there anything else I can get for you?" he asked as he removed their plates.

Derick looked to Siobhan. "You like cannolis?"

"Is there anyone who doesn't?"

"Two?" the waiter asked.

"Please," Derick said. "And I'll take a cup of coffee." He gestured to Siobhan. "Tea?"

She nodded. "Any hot herbal tea you have would be great."

The waiter nodded and headed back toward the small bar at the back of the restaurant. The place was beautiful and intimate.

There were maybe fifteen tables sprinkled around the cozy space. Two of the walls were made of weathered-looking, exposed brick.

Siobhan couldn't resist looking around in awe. "If I didn't know better, I'd think I were actually in Italy."

Derick sat back in his chair, his fitted black polo stretching across his muscular chest. She found herself picturing what his chest looked like beneath his shirt. Just the right amount of hair on his pecs, some leading down his chiseled abs to where the top of his tight boxer briefs hugged his hip—

"When were you there last?"

Huh? It took her a moment to remember what they'd been talking about. She tried to regain her composure before speaking, though she could feel the embarrassment heating her cheeks. "Italy? Never, actually. I really only know what I've seen in pictures and movies. I'd love to go, though. As an aspiring artist, I feel like I should eventually take a trip there."

"Only 'aspiring'? You seemed pretty good to me."

Siobhan put her elbow on the table and plopped her head into her hand. "Thank you. But I need to actually sell some of my art before I drop the 'aspiring.' Which will hopefully be soon. A few of my paintings will be in a gallery that's opening in a few weeks."

Derick's face lit up. He looked genuinely impressed. "Really? That's exciting."

Siobhan inhaled a shaky breath. Just the thought of strangers judging whether her art was worth something made her jittery. "It's exciting, but every time I think about it, I feel like I'm going to pass out."

"Well don't do that, because then you'll miss dessert," Derick said, gesturing to the waiter who was approaching with their cannolis and drinks.

Siobhan leaned back in her seat so the server could place her plate and tea in front of her. "I won't really faint. But it does make me nervous thinking about it. I'm such a cliché. I moved here because it's where everyone goes to pursue their dreams, you know?"

Derick nodded.

"But now that I'm here, I have to admit that New York intimidates me a little," she continued.

"It's just like any other city," Derick replied, though she was sure he was just trying to make her feel better. He put some sugar in his coffee and stirred it. "When did you move here?"

"The middle of March. So I've been here almost four months. But I've been so busy, I haven't gotten to really see much of the city yet. Though I've seen enough to know that it's a far cry from Oklahoma."

Siobhan saw a spark of excitement in Derick's eyes. He ran a hand across the short, dark hair on his face, and Siobhan wondered how it would feel against her skin. "What do you say we take dessert to go?"

Siobhan narrowed her eyes in confusion. "Okay?" she said as more of a question than an answer.

Derick quickly pulled out his wallet and put two hundred dollars on the table, which Siobhan was certain was way too much for what they'd just eaten, even with a generous tip included. "Ready?" he asked, picking up his cannoli.

Siobhan nodded, grabbing her dessert and following him out to the street, where he began walking. She hurried to keep up with him.

"First thing you need to know about being a New Yorker is how to eat on the go. You have to walk with a purpose. Even if you don't really have one."

Siobhan lifted her cannoli to her mouth. "Doesn't seem that difficult," she said before taking a bite.

Derick raised his eyebrows as he chewed. "This coming from someone I picked up off the floor when we first met."

Siobhan gave him a playful slap to his arm. "That's not true! You caught me before I hit the ground."

They continued on for five minutes or so, weaving around other people. "Where are we going?" Siobhan asked.

"You'll see," Derick replied. "We're practically there." He pointed ahead to a sleek building that seemed to be made up entirely of windows. Siobhan recognized the famous acronym on the side. "The Museum of Modern Art," she said, more to herself than to Derick.

"Yup. You know about art, and I know about New York. I figured it would be a good place to start."

"Start what?"

"Your tour," Derick answered, holding the door so she could enter.

"My tour?" she asked, her head drifting back so she could look up at the expansive space. Even the lobby of the museum looked like a piece of art—clean lines, high ceilings, marble and glass surrounding them.

"Your tour of New York." He grinned broadly.

Siobhan looked at her watch. "But it's almost six. Isn't the museum closed?"

"Not for us, it's not."

Chapter 7

AFTER DERICK PASSED the security guard a handful of crisp bills, Siobhan did her best to show him paintings by some of the more well-known artists: Matisse, Pollock, Monet.

"This is one of my favorites," Siobhan said, pointing to *The Persistence of Memory* by Salvador Dalí.

"I've seen this one. It was in my high school Spanish book."

Siobhan laughed. "I think it was in mine too, actually. But I've loved it even before then. When I first started to get interested in art, I used to check out books from the library on different artists and read about the paintings."

"Nerd," he elbowed her playfully. "So what did the book say about these lumpy clocks?"

Siobhan laughed again. "The *melting* clocks. There are a bunch of theories. Some people thought it had to do with Einstein's Theory of Relativity, but Dalí denied that. I like the idea that it could mean that time is an abstract concept. It's not concrete, but it isn't nonexistent, either. It lies somewhere in the middle of the two."

Derick looked from her to the painting and then back at her again.

"Time is something created by humans," she continued. "We have to follow a schedule, be somewhere at a certain time—no other species believes that. In a sense, we made it up. But time is also very real. That's what makes every moment special. Once it's gone, you can never get it back."

Shrugging, she paused for a few seconds. "Except in your memory or a dream, maybe." She gazed at the painting, barely able to believe she was looking at the real thing. "I think that's why I like surrealism so much. It's where fiction and reality meet. It's also something I could never paint myself. So that alone impresses me."

"I don't *get* it—how people critique art. It's like another language. One that I don't speak. It's interesting though, at least when *you* talk about it." He let his eyes drift away from the painting as he turned to face her. "Though if I'm looking at anything in this building, I'd much rather it be you."

Siobhan felt the rush of heat to her cheeks as Derick's caramel-colored eyes raked over her entire body. She'd noticed him do that earlier, his gaze fixed on Siobhan as if he were there to admire her and not the masterpieces surrounding them. Though she was fully clothed, it somehow made her feel exposed.

But she didn't mind it. She actually liked that Derick looked as though he might eat her alive at any moment. She desperately wanted him to.

He took a step closer and placed a hand on her cheek. The gentle touch sent a spark of electricity pulsing through her body. "Kiss me," she said.

Though the request had come from Siobhan's own mouth, it still surprised her. She usually wasn't this forward. But if she had to stand this close to Derick again without his lips pressed against hers, she felt like she might implode.

There was something about this man that had her wanting to act rather than think, to feel rather than suppress. Before meeting Derick, she'd only felt this kind of passion for art. But Derick ignited a fire inside her that she couldn't put out even if she wanted to. And she definitely didn't want to.

Derick's eyes grew wide in what she recognized as the same desire she felt in herself. "Follow me." His voice sounded as if he'd been gargling with pebbles as he grabbed her hand and led her into a dimly lit room.

As soon as they turned the corner, he was on her, pushing her against the wall in the blessedly empty room. She hoped it indicated the things to come. She didn't want gentle. She wanted him to ravish her.

Their mouths moved wildly as a growl escaped from low in Derick's chest. The sound caused her core to tighten. She was lit up with sensation, an overwhelming need to claim this man who had turned her inside out. Time seemed to slow as neither moved to take things further. The kiss was enough. It was everything.

But eventually, the heat simmering between them called

for more. His mouth left hers, and he nuzzled into her neck, his facial hair tickling her skin as he sucked hungrily on her flesh. Her body seemed to melt against his.

"I love the way you taste," Derick rasped against her skin.

Her response was a soft moan that she released on an exhale as Derick's hand skated up her flowing, navy-blue tank. *Even the things he says are hot.*

"This okay?" he asked.

"Mm-hmm. More than okay." She inhaled deeply, trying to take in as much of him as possible. The smell of soap mingled with the hint of sweat on his skin—a combination she thought she'd never get enough of.

As his hips ground against her, she felt his erection on her abdomen. She brought her lips back to his and lost herself in the kiss.

She wanted him to keep going, ease the wet ache between her thighs that had been there since last night. She was sure this would be enough if she wrapped her leg around him and he kept the pressure right where she needed it.

"We should probably take this somewhere else," Derick said, pulling back slightly and looking around. "I'm not sure I can keep doing this with that statue of David watching."

Siobhan glanced at the two-foot-tall sculpture Derick was pointing to. "That's definitely not David."

"It's the statue of some naked guy. That's close enough." Derick put a finger under her chin and gently lifted up her head to make eye contact.

God, he's gorgeous.

"My place?" he asked softly before giving her a light kiss.

Siobhan let out an audible exhale. "I can't."

Derick looked apologetic. "I didn't mean… We don't have to…"

"Oh no. That's not what I meant. I want to. Like really, really want to. You have no idea."

Glancing down at his cock still straining against his khaki shorts, Derick gave her an amused grin. "I'm pretty sure I have *some* idea."

"Right." She shook her head as if trying to clear it. "I just can't right *now*. I need to pick up my neighbor's daughter from gymnastics and then start getting ready for work."

Derick cocked his head to the side and put his hands on her biceps. "I don't feel like that's going to be as much fun for you as what I had planned."

"Probably not," she said, deflated. As the two of them straightened their clothes, the heat between them cooled just enough to make Siobhan thankful that they couldn't take things any further. She liked Derick and was interested in knowing more about him than just what he looked like naked.

Chapter 8

SIOBHAN SHIFTED IN her seat, a mixture of discomfort and excitement coursing through her. She and Derick decided to meet up on the following Tuesday since Siobhan didn't have to work, and they wouldn't be combating tourists visiting for the weekend. Derick had picked her up at 8:00 a.m., greeting her with a smile and a driver standing beside a black Escalade. At least that's what Siobhan thought it was called.

Derick explained that he had a lot planned, starting with a quick stop to his favorite coffeehouse before they headed to the Statue of Liberty. He seemed so excited, Siobhan was surprised he wasn't vibrating.

"I figured we'd eat quickly and then begin our tour." Derick smiled as he spoke, and Siobhan calmed at the sight of it.

On their way to the ferry after breakfast, Derick pointed out some of the local sights, most of which Siobhan still hadn't seen. Derick explained that he'd tried to hire a boat to take them out to Liberty Island, but only the ferries were allowed to dock there. He'd already reserved their tickets, and

Siobhan was flattered by how much forethought he'd put into the day, though she was thrown a little off-center by the idea that he'd tried to hire a private boat to get them to the island.

Siobhan tried to maintain her excitement, but Derick's apparent wealth was distracting her. She'd known Derick had money. The Stone Room was renowned for attracting wealthy men. But Derick had never seemed like the men who frequented the place. He seemed down to earth. More like her.

But, as they began to climb the 377 steps to the crown of Lady Liberty, she was thinking less about Derick's attempted indulgence and more about how she wished she'd done more cardio since moving to New York.

After they'd looked around for a bit, and Derick had bought her a stuffed replica of the Statue of Liberty, they caught the ferry back and continued their tour.

They arrived at the Empire State Building a little while later. The elevator was crammed with people as it ascended the 102 stories. Derick put his back flush against the wall and pulled Siobhan to stand in front of him. He left his hands on her hips, and she couldn't resist leaning back into him.

"Maybe we should just spend the day on this elevator," he whispered.

She turned her head so she could see him out of the corner of her eye. "I don't think that's what I was promised when I accepted this date."

The elevator *dinged* as they reached their destination. Derick sighed as he grabbed her hand and threaded his fingers through hers. "Guess I'd better keep my promise. Come on," he added with a smirk.

They walked around the observation deck for a bit, looking through the coin-operated binoculars. Derick held something out to her.

"What's this?" she said, as he dropped the object in her palm.

"A penny."

She laughed. "What am I supposed to do with this?"

"Drop it over the ledge," he said, as if it were obvious.

She narrowed her eyes and looked at the coin in her hand. "Why?"

"Because it'll kill someone."

Siobhan's eyes flew up to his. "What?" She may have said it a little loudly, because all of the people in their vicinity turned to stare at them.

Derick, the bastard, just started laughing. "You've never heard that urban legend?"

"That it's customary to commit homicide when visiting the Empire State Building? No. I must've missed that one."

He laughed again. "People used to say that if you threw a penny from this high up that it'd kill someone if it hit them. *Mythbusters* disproved that theory though. But it's still supposed to grant you a wish." He ran his fingers over the fence in front of them. "Too bad you can't actually throw the pennies over anymore. We'll have to settle for leaving them on the ledge."

Siobhan toyed with the penny in her palm. "I don't believe in wishes. I make my own luck," she said with a wink, even though she meant every word.

"Suit yourself," Derick said, as he closed his eyes and was still for a second before putting his penny on the ledge. He looked at Siobhan. "You're going to be sad when I get my wish, and you don't get yours."

"What was your wish?"

"Drop your penny, and I'll tell you."

"That's blackmail," she grumbled. But she complied anyway, wishing that her upcoming show would be profitable. She nearly laughed out loud at her wish. Then she placed the penny on the ledge and put her hands on her hips. She turned to face Derick again. "Okay, fess up."

Derick moved closer to her, and the baby-blue T-shirt he was wearing brushed up against her white tank top. His hands wrapped around her waist as she slid hers up to wrap around his neck. "To kiss you on top of the Empire State Building."

Before she could reply, his lips were on hers. The kiss was gentle, a slow glide that was electrifying in its sweetness. She wanted more. She always wanted more with him.

Too soon, he was pulling back, and her body craved his with an intensity she hadn't felt with anyone before. "Why are we always somewhere public when I kiss you?"

"Not sure. But it's a trend we should stop." Siobhan was embarrassed by how breathless her reply sounded.

"What was your wish?" he asked.

Siobhan hesitated a moment. She didn't want to tell Derick her wish—whether because she didn't want to admit how greedy she was or because she didn't want to jinx it, she wasn't quite sure. "If I tell you it won't come true," she said with a smile that she hoped would convince him she was kidding.

"I told you and mine still came true."

"I like to play it safe."

They looked at each other for a moment longer before Derick nodded, took her hand, and led her to the lobby.

"Are you averse to food carts?" Derick asked as they exited the building.

"Food carts? Um, no. Why?"

"Because I figured a tour of New York wouldn't be complete without getting food from one. And I know of a really good one."

They ate lunch as they walked past the buildings. She was so caught up in the New York scenery, she hadn't even noticed they'd arrived at the Rockefeller Center ice skating rink until Derick asked her if she could skate.

Siobhan couldn't help but laugh. "No. I'm way too uncoordinated to skate."

"Well, this is a New York City must. You have to get on the ice once the rink reopens."

"So not happening." She turned toward him and realized how close they were standing. Almost as close as they'd been at the Empire State Building.

He looked at her intently as he tucked some of her hair behind her shoulder. "I've already kept you from falling once. Trust me to do it again."

Staring into his amber-colored eyes, she felt goose bumps break out across her skin. His eyes lowered to her mouth, and she couldn't resist darting her tongue out to moisten her lips. "Okay. I trust you."

His smile was dazzling as he leaned in and kissed her.

It wasn't a long kiss, just a quick taste. Then they both looked back at the rink for a few minutes without speaking. And it was a good quiet—full of contentment.

Chapter 9

AFTER ROCKEFELLER CENTER, they'd walked around New York, stopping and looking at things as they caught their fancy. Siobhan enjoyed taking in the city. But at seven, Derick called for the car to come pick them up and take them to dinner.

"Is this where we're eating?" she asked as the car stopped in front of Le Parker Meridien Hotel.

"Yup," Derick replied as he climbed out of the backseat. He stretched out his hand and helped her out of the car. "Ever been here?"

"Nope." They walked toward the entrance hand in hand. But as soon as they entered the foyer, Siobhan stopped dead. "We can't eat here," she said, panic coursing through her at the thought of dining in the elegant hotel. She would have never been in this situation if Derick had just been a normal guy and not someone she'd met at the Stone Room. He'd wanted to charter a private boat for part of their tour and now he was taking her here for dinner. Clearly he had money. Lots of it.

Derick's eyebrows pinched together. "We can't?"

Siobhan took in the marble floors, then her gaze climbed up the white columns, and finally landed on the frescoed ceiling. "No. We look like hobos."

Derick simply smiled and tugged on her hand, pulling her after him as he walked past the concierge desk and down a hall.

"Derick, I'm serious." She tried to pull free, but he wasn't letting go.

Despite the fact that she was allowing him to lead her through the hotel, she wasn't happy about it. She was rigid behind him. But that didn't stop Derick from leading her toward their destination. He stopped and waved his hand at the restaurant in front of him. "Welcome to the Burger Joint."

She looked at her surroundings and took a deep breath to try to calm herself. But then she realized that the restaurant wasn't fancy at all. It was exactly what the name suggested.

He led her to one of the brown leather booths against the wood-paneled wall that was covered in colored writing. They slid in across from each other. "Yeah. It looks like a hole in the wall," Derick said, "but it has phenomenal burgers. I figured it'd be better to go somewhere casual since we've been walking around all day."

She looked at the line for ordering and let the sense of relief wash over her. "This place is awesome. I was craving a burger."

"Oh, good. They only have burgers and fries, so I was really hoping I didn't go wrong."

"It's perfect."

Derick smiled. "I'll go up and order them while you save our seats. Want anything specific on your burger?"

"I'll eat anything, so just order two of whatever you're having," Siobhan replied.

Derick got up to place their orders and returned quickly with a pitcher of Sam Adams. He poured them both a pint and then sat back.

They stared at each other for a second. "I can't believe a place like this is in here," Siobhan finally said.

"So I gathered from your strong resistance in the lobby."

"Yeah, I thought you were leading me to a five-star restaurant. There was no way I was sitting in a formal dining room wearing a tank top and sneakers."

Derick took a sip of his beer. "Nah, but we can go somewhere nice next time. This seemed to fit the day better."

"Definitely," Siobhan agreed.

Their order was called quickly so Derick went to retrieve it. When he came back they both dug in—all conversation on hold for the time being.

Eventually, Siobhan put down her burger. "That's it. I'm stuffed."

Derick laughed. They looked at each other for a second while Siobhan fiddled with her napkin. As perfect as the day had been, there was something she needed to say.

"So I had a great time today, and it was really nice of you to do all this for me. But I'm a pretty simple girl. We don't have to go on these extravagant dates."

Derick looked confused. "But you said you had a great time."

"I did. But I can have fun without spending a lot of money. This must have cost so much. A tour of the city, a private driver. You even said you were going to charter a boat."

"It's not a big deal." He shrugged. "I like you, and I have the money."

Siobhan had been wondering when Derick's financial status might come up. She knew if he frequented the Stone Room that he had money. She just wasn't sure how much. She took another sip of her beer and tried to relax. "What is it you do for a living?"

Derick clasped his hands on the table. "I'm a consultant for app developers."

"Oh, wow." Siobhan was interested. It seemed like a unique career, and maybe he didn't have as much money as she originally thought. There couldn't be *that* much money in consulting. "How did you get into that?"

"In college, a couple buddies and I were talking at a bar one night—we'd been drinking, which made the concept seem even better—and we came up with an idea for an app. One of my friends was getting a degree in computer programming so he built it, we all helped launch it, it took off, and we ended up selling it a few years ago. But we have stock and it's still paying dividends."

Siobhan leaned forward as if prompting him to continue. When he didn't elaborate, she asked, "What does it do?"

"It's stupid really. It's called the Bar Tab. It allows you to check-in at a bar and rate different aspects of it: the cost of drinks, approximate guy-to-girl ratio, entertainment, attractiveness of the customers, that kind of stuff. It's all pretty superficial, but people liked using it. When bars caught on that they could use it for promotions the whole thing really took off. The app eventually caught the attention of a social networking site who offered to buy the rights to it. We were tired of running it, fixing glitches, promoting, all that kind of stuff, so we were happy to sell. Now I consult with other app developers, which is nice because it's something I know a lot about, and I can set my own hours."

Siobhan looked down at the table. "There's usually crazy money in that stuff, isn't there? Selling apps?"

"There's some. There were three of us, so we had to split it. We also had a lot of college debt, but I made enough to be comfortable."

Siobhan nodded. She felt herself go quiet but tried not to seem overly bothered by the revelation.

They left soon after and Derick had the driver take them back through Times Square. Siobhan was in awe of the lights and activity, causing whatever unease that had been between them to evaporate. He stared at her as the lights splashed her face in color and reflected off the diamond stud earrings she often wore.

He insisted on walking her to her door even though she

said she'd be fine. Once they got to her apartment, Derick used his body to ease her back against the door. He seemed to watch her for any signs that she wanted him to stop, but she didn't give him one. She wanted this. And as Derick wrapped a hand around her nape and kissed the hell out of her, she knew he wanted it just as much, too.

His hands roved all over her body: moving from her nape down over the swell of her breasts, before rucking up her tank top so he could grip the soft skin on her hip.

Her hands were equally greedy as they pulled up his shirt so her fingers could trace over his bare chest.

On some level, Siobhan realized they were getting a little carried away as they stood in her hallway, but she couldn't bring herself to stop. His tongue tangled with hers as he ground his hard cock against her belly.

She gasped, which allowed him to take the kiss deeper. She wanted him to consume her. His hands found the button on her shorts and undid it.

Pushing gently against his chest, she felt herself become breathless. Then she eased back from him slightly, put her key in the door, and unlocked it. "You coming?"

Hell yes.

Once they were in the door and had closed it behind them, they were on each other, picking up where they had left off. Derick pressed his body against hers, causing her back to lean against the door.

He pushed under her shirt again, but this time he kept lifting until he freed her body from it. As he licked and kissed a trail from her neck down to her collarbone, Siobhan felt herself losing control.

Her hands went to his pants, unbuckling his belt and popping the button. She lowered the zipper and he helped push them down his hips until gravity took over the job.

Derick's hands squeezed her breasts over her bra before moving south, undoing her shorts, and pushing his hand between her skin and the soft fabric of her underwear. He found her clit and massaged it gently yet urgently, as her smooth hand gripped the even smoother skin of his cock.

She dragged her fist up and down his length, hoping that it was fast enough to get him close, but slow enough to edge him on the brink of climax without pushing him over.

She panted and groaned with pleasure, knowing she was close to falling apart as she rode his fingers. He massaged her clit with his thumb as he pulled her shorts down with his free hand before thrusting his index finger inside her.

As he continued fingering her, she became more frantic. Her hand gripped his cock tighter and moved quicker. Siobhan dug the nails of her other hand into his bicep as her climax drew closer.

Finally she moaned loudly, her body shaking with her release. Her orgasm caused her hand to clamp even tighter around him, which brought on his orgasm.

His cum shot all over her bare belly as his body tightened with pleasure. She felt his thighs shaking with the release, and as she looked down, she couldn't help the primal satisfaction she felt because he'd marked her.

The sight made her want him to do it again.

He leaned in to kiss her, this time more gently as they both came down from the sexual high. Kissing his way up to her ear, he whispered, "Can I stay?"

Chapter 10

"SO THEN WHAT?" Cory asked.

Siobhan shrugged. "Then nothing."

"So let me get this straight," Cory said. "You let a smokin' hot guy get you off against your door, but you didn't let him stay the night?"

"No." Siobhan let out a deflated sigh, rested her elbows against the smooth bar, and propped her chin on her hands. She knew it sounded crazy that she didn't let him stay, especially considering how far they had already taken things, but she still felt like she'd made the right decision.

Siobhan noticed Blaine's eyes widen in the mirror behind the bar as she finished reapplying her lip gloss. "So you *don't* want to have sex with Derick Miller?" She turned around to face the girls again.

"Of course I *want* to have sex with him. Have you seen him?" Not able to stay seated a moment longer, she stood and walked a few feet away, needing to release some of her nervous energy. "I know we've already taken it pretty far, but any further felt…too fast. I don't want to seem like one of those chicks who falls into bed with a guy just because he's wealthy."

"Why not? It worked for Tiffany." Cory pointed over at the petite redhead who was typing on one of the restaurant's iPads, and the girls laughed.

Siobhan didn't know whether Cory was kidding. "Are you serious?"

"Yeah, I'm serious. You think those torpedoes are real? She looks like Raggedy Ann on growth hormones."

Siobhan knew Tiffany's breasts were fake, but it had never occurred to her that she'd gotten them because of her job. She felt her jaw drop. "She had sex with a customer, and he paid for them?"

Marnel shook her head. "Nope. She had sex with a customer, and he put them in. He was some famous plastic surgeon out in LA."

Siobhan lowered her voice and flung an arm in Tiffany's direction. "See? That's exactly what I'm saying. I'm not using Derick like that, and I don't want anyone thinking I am. His money makes me uncomfortable. To be honest, I kind of wish he didn't even have it. It just complicates things."

Cory looked confused. "How does money complicate things? It would make all of our lives easier." She paused, probably waiting for someone to agree with her. "What if the situation were reversed? Your dream is to sell your paintings and make a living off your art eventually. If that happens, I'm sure you wouldn't want some guy judging you just because you had money."

"I'm not *judging* him. Besides, that's different."

"How?"

"Because…" Siobhan trailed off.

Blaine finished putting the last of the coasters on the bar and looked at her. "We're not in first grade so 'because' isn't a sufficient explanation. Try again."

Siobhan remained quiet, lost in her thoughts. She wasn't sure *how* it was different. She just knew it was. Fidgeting with her silver bracelet, she tried to put her feelings into words. "Because I've been painting my whole life. I moved out here with no help from anyone, and I work my ass off so I can stay." She could feel herself getting defensive, though she didn't know why. "Derick created an app when he was in college and sold the idea for God knows how much. He made it sound so *easy*. And I don't begrudge him that. I'm glad he's successful. But if I'm ever lucky enough to support myself doing what I love, it'll be because I sacrificed a lot of my time and energy making it happen. It won't have come easy for me."

The girls stared silently at her, but they looked empathetic. Marnel was the first to speak. "So…what? You're just not going to see him anymore because he has money?"

"No." Siobhan sighed, bringing her hair around to rest in front of her shoulder. "I'm going to give it a shot. He seems sweet, and he's funny, and he looks like a bearded god." She felt a goofy grin spread across her face. "I just want to take things slowly. That's all."

"You want to take things slowly?" Cory sounded unconvinced. "With the bearded god who felt you up in an art museum and finger-banged you against a door?"

Siobhan shrugged. "Yeah. It'll be fine."

Chapter 11

DERICK SWEPT A hand across his brow to wipe the sweat away. It was at least ninety degrees, and the humidity made it feel even hotter. He was thankful for the shade that the tall trees provided. He and Siobhan had walked about a mile and a half to the little city dog park, picking up four small dogs on the way.

He was already exhausted. It wasn't that he was out of shape. He worked out five times a week. But that was when he wanted to sweat. This was something entirely different. They'd spent the past ten minutes trying to corral the two beagle puppies and get them leashed again while the white toy poodle and...whatever the long-haired yappy one was called waited on their leashes attached to a nearby pole.

"Stay there," Derick called to Siobhan, who was stationed near a tree. "I'm going to chase her, and when she runs by, grab her." Siobhan nodded, and Derick lunged, forcing the dog to run right past the tree.

When she did, Siobhan snatched her up. "Gotcha," she

said. Then she gave the dog a little kiss on her brown and white face.

Derick assumed the brother of the recently captured dog must have just lost interest in the one-sided game because a few minutes later, he wandered over to the other three, finally ready to get back on his leash. "I can't believe you do this on your own three times a week," Derick said, taking a long swig from his water bottle and then holding it on the back of his neck.

Siobhan shrugged. "Dog walking in New York is good money. And I only take them to the park every now and then. I've never let the puppies off their leashes before. I didn't know they'd be that crazy."

Derick laughed. "I never thought something with six-inch legs could outrun me." After giving the dogs some water, he held the gate open for Siobhan to walk through with the beagles. Then he followed with the other two, thankful that their little chore would be coming to an end soon and they could have some time to themselves. Or so he hoped.

Over the course of the few weeks that they'd been seeing each other, it always felt like their time together was getting cut short. Siobhan was always running off to get ready to go into the Stone Room for the night, or racing home so she could babysit for one of her neighbor's kids.

Derick felt bad that she was always so busy. Especially when he was always so *not* busy. "You want to grab some ice cream after we drop off the dogs?" he asked. He lifted the bottom of his T-shirt up and maneuvered it over his head, wiping the sweat off his face and neck before draping the shirt over his shoulder.

He caught Siobhan's gaze drift to his chest and then a little lower as she seemed to appraise him. "Sure. Ice cream sounds good," she said. "I just have to get back home by two or so because I have a student coming over."

Derick smiled. "Is it one of my girlfriends from your art class?"

Siobhan laughed and pulled back on the dogs' leashes. "No, not an art student. I tutor a few kids in English. This one will be a high school sophomore in September. He lives down the hall from me."

Derick nodded. "Oh."

"His family moved here from Mali," she continued. "French is his first language, but his parents want him to try to improve his English over the summer. They can't pay me much, but every little bit helps. And he actually seems like he's learning something, so I kind of like it."

They walked a little farther in silence as Derick decided what to say. He'd been hoping that since she was working at the Stone Room tonight, they could at least spend the day together.

"What's wrong?" Siobhan asked, obviously sensing his disappointment.

Derick shrugged. "Nothing's *wrong* really. I just like being with you, and you're always doing all these odd jobs. It cuts into our time together."

Siobhan slowed down a little and looked over at him. "I like spending time with you, too, but it's work. I don't have much of a choice."

On some level Derick understood that. People worked. But there was no reason Siobhan had to do so many little jobs that probably paid next to nothing instead of spending time with him. She was sacrificing her life for work. And that was something Derick really didn't like, especially if he could help.

He'd watched his mother work for years to support him and his older brother. And since she'd passed away before Derick had made his money, he'd never gotten the chance to give her the life she'd always tried so hard to give to him. He didn't want to watch someone else he cared about do the same thing. "You always have a choice. Tell the kid you aren't tutoring anymore."

Derick heard how casual his statement sounded, and Siobhan's expression, combined with the fact that she'd stopped abruptly, told him she'd picked up on his tone, too. And she didn't look happy.

"And what do I tell my landlord? That I was spending time with Derick Miller so he'll just have to excuse the late rent?"

"How much will you be short?"

She narrowed her eyes at him. "What?"

"If you skip tutoring? How much would you need?"

She shook her head slowly, and her jaw tensed. "Don't even say what I think—"

"It can't be much if a few sessions would've covered it." He could tell that comment only irritated her, so he tried to correct it. "I wasn't going to pay the whole thing, just whatever—"

"I don't need your money." Siobhan looked him up and down. But this time her eyes didn't hold admiration as they had when he'd taken off his shirt a few blocks back. This time they held disgust. "And I definitely don't need this." Then she started walking again.

"I know you don't *need* my money. I just—"

"You just what, Derick? Wanted to make me feel inadequate? Make me feel like I'm incapable of taking care of myself? Congratulations. Mission accomplished."

Derick sped up to catch her. He felt horrible. "No. I wasn't trying to do either of those things. I wanted to make your life easier. That's all. So you don't have to work as hard."

She stopped again, and turned to face him. This time her disgust had morphed into anger. "And what makes you think that I don't want to work hard?"

Derick was silent.

"I know this isn't true in *your* world, but in mine, hard work is the only way you'll ever make anything of yourself. So maybe I don't want it to be easy. Have you ever thought of that?" She reached over and grabbed the leashes he'd been holding. "And for the record, you're not making this"—she gestured between them with her free hand—"You're not making this easy, either."

Then she walked away. And this time Derick knew better than to chase after her.

Chapter 12

SIOBHAN FINISHED COUNTING out her tips for the night and put the money into her purse. *Not bad for a Sunday night.* She closed the oversized bag, headed over to the bar to say good-bye to the girls, and then made her way toward the exit. She hadn't told them about her fight with Derick. She didn't think she needed to. He hadn't been in the bar since their fight a few days ago, and she hadn't been in the most jovial of moods.

Derick had left two messages asking her to call him. She thought that she would've calmed down by now—enough to call him back at least—but her anger had only grown. How dare he offer to give her money as if she wasn't capable of earning it on her own? The gesture had been insulting.

Siobhan slid off her heels and slipped on a pair of flip flops, tossing the uncomfortable footwear into her bag before pulling open the heavy glass door to the street. She took a deep breath, inhaling the thick muggy air as she let the door close softly behind her.

She'd just adjusted her bag on her shoulder when she heard him speak from behind her.

"You haven't returned any of my calls. Can I talk to you for a minute?"

Siobhan let out an annoyed huff, but she didn't respond.

"I want you to try to hear what I have to say. Please."

She turned to face him, which caused his masculine features to soften.

Derick sighed. "I shouldn't have offered to pay some of your rent. I know you work hard. And there's a lot of pride in that. It wasn't my intention to take that away from you."

"Well that's good because my pride isn't something you have the power to take."

Derick rubbed a hand across his forehead and dropped his gaze to the sidewalk before bringing it back up to meet hers. He looked contrite. "I have a lot of money."

Siobhan rolled her eyes.

"And it wasn't really hard to come by. At least not through what I'd consider hard work. I put in a lot of hours when the app was just getting started, but we made most of the money when we sold the company. And that part was easy." He shrugged. "I just got lucky. The right idea at the right time sold to the right company for the right amount of money."

Her eyes narrowed at him. "How perfect for you."

"I didn't mean it like that." Derick's posture deflated slightly. "Even though I still work consulting with app developers, I can make my own hours. And since it's something I like doing, it doesn't feel like work. That's why it didn't seem like a big deal to offer you some money so I could see you more and so you could cut back."

"But it is a big deal. I didn't earn that money. You did," she said, her voice somehow calm, though she felt anything but. "It doesn't matter how you got it. It's still yours."

"You're right. It is mine. So I should be able to do whatever I want with it. Siobhan, I'm not sure you know this, in fact I'm sure you don't, but with everything all totaled I'm worth over a billion dollars." He said it with such conviction, like it should comfort her somehow. "What would I do with all of that? I know my money makes you uncomfortable, and to be honest, it makes me a little uncomfortable, too. That's why I downplayed how much I had at dinner. I didn't want it to come between us."

"Well, you didn't do a very good job of that."

She turned and took a few steps to leave, but Derick caught her arm. "Siobhan, I have more money than I know what to do with and an equal amount of time on my hands. And it's time I want to spend with you. Just let me help."

She felt her body go rigid, her arm tense in his hand. She jerked it free and turned around to look him in the eyes. "Yeah, well I don't need your help. And more than that, I don't want it."

As she walked away from him for the second time in less than a week, she suppressed the urge to take one final look at the man she likely would never see again.

Chapter 13

TAKING A DEEP BREATH of the thick summer air, Derick leaned against the stucco exterior of the Brooklyn apartment building. Finally, after a half hour or so, someone opened the main door, allowing Derick to enter behind them.

He ascended the two flights of stairs to Siobhan's apartment and knocked confidently, though he didn't feel it. He knew she didn't want to see him, and he didn't know exactly what he was going to say. That is, if she even let him speak.

His mind ran through the list of possibilities. Maybe she'd curse him out. Maybe she'd shut the door on him. Maybe she'd see him through the peephole and pretend she wasn't home. Even though the music he could hear coming from inside told him differently. Or maybe…

Holy shit. Derick felt his jaw lower at the sight of her.

Maybe she'd open the door looking hot as hell in a pale-green paint-splattered tank top, her hair pulled up into the same messy hairstyle she'd worn in the park that day.

She eyed Derick warily and blew a stray strand of hair

away from her face. "You don't quit, do you?" Her tone sounded annoyed, but her body language didn't match it. Siobhan grabbed a remote from a nearby table and lowered the music, which he now recognized as Adele. Siobhan raised a curious eyebrow at him. Her long legs seemed to extend even farther in her cutoff jean shorts as she leaned against the doorframe.

Derick was suddenly reminded that he should be speaking. "I was an asshole," he blurted out. "I understand if you don't want to see me. Though I hope you still do. But even if you don't, I still think you deserve a proper apology." God, he sounded like a moron. "No excuses."

Derick wished Siobhan would let him help her. It would make things easier for both of them. But even though he didn't fully agree with her choice, he was willing to concede that one point if it meant she might give him another shot.

Siobhan tilted her head to the side and rested it against the faded beige molding. "I'm listening."

Her voice seemed to have softened a bit, and Derick was thankful. He drew in a breath and thought about what to say. "I'm sorry for offering to give you money. And I'm sorry for not listening to you. As you've probably noticed, I can be a little clueless sometimes. But my intention was only to help, never to hurt. I'd never want to do that. I was a jerk, and I'm hoping you can forgive me." He'd been watching for a sign that she'd accepted his apology—a glimmer in her eye, a small lift on the corner of her lips. So far she hadn't given him one.

But she was letting him talk. That was something. "I have a proposition for you," he continued.

Siobhan toyed with the paintbrush she'd been holding. "A proposition?" And then he saw it—the amused narrowing of her eyes. She was giving him an opening.

Derick slid his hands into his pockets, feeling a little more at ease now. "Yeah. I thought we could start over from the beginning. You know, since I'm an idiot who screwed up a perfectly good thing."

He thought he recognized the beginning of a smile on Siobhan's lips. "And why would I want to start over with an idiot?"

Derick shrugged, the corner of his own lips lifting slightly, too. "Because I'm handsome?" he answered, repeating the words he said when he'd asked her to lunch the first time.

Her soft laugh told him she remembered. "So we're going to start over?" she asked. "Just like that?"

"Mm-hmm." He said it as if it were simple. He hoped it would be.

Her eyes narrowed again. She looked like she was trying to figure him out. She released a long breath and dropped her arms so they hung by her sides. "I think we need to clear up a few things first."

Derick tried to resist the urge to fidget.

"Despite the world's apparent fascination with Julia Roberts, I'm not looking for a Richard Gere to ride in on his limo, climb my balcony, and rescue me from my life. I'm my own savior, Derick. I want a partner. Not a sugar daddy. Can you handle that?"

Derick didn't hesitate. He'd promise her anything. "Yes."

She scrutinized him for a moment. "Okay," she finally said, her posture opening as she extended a hand to him. "I'm Siobhan."

Derick gave her a genuine smile of relief. "Siobhan. That's a beautiful name," he said. "I'm Derick."

They held hands for a moment, as if the physical contact conducted whatever seemed to pass between them as they stared into each other's eyes. Eventually Siobhan let go and gestured into her apartment. "You want to come in, Derick?"

He wanted to say yes, but he knew he shouldn't. He'd made it this far and didn't want to fuck things up again. "You know, it's not really a good idea to invite strangers into your apartment."

Siobhan bit her bottom lip. "You're probably right."

"Besides," Derick added. "You look like you're working." He pointed past her to the canvas. "So I should probably let you get back to it."

She nodded. "I appreciate that."

"But give me a call when you get a moment. I'd love to take you out for coffee sometime."

She shook her head and let out a quiet laugh. "I'm actually more of a tea girl."

Derick nodded. "Good to know," he said, before turning to leave. He took a few steps before glancing back at her. She was still leaning against the doorway, giving him that sexy stare he'd missed so much. He momentarily considered accepting her invitation. But instead he said, "It was nice meeting you, Siobhan. Have a good day."

She smiled broadly as she tapped the handle of the paintbrush against her fingers. "You too, Derick."

Chapter 14

"WHEREVER I WANT to go?" Siobhan asked as they sat in the back of the Escalade.

Derick nodded. He'd almost planned their date, but then reconsidered. He and Siobhan had been all over the city, but he'd never actually asked her where she wanted to go.

"You're sure?" She dragged the syllables out, a glint of mischief in her eyes. Maybe he should've taken her to the Russian Tea Room after all.

"You're making me nervous," he said. "Just tell me."

"Coney Island. I've heard about it a bunch of times but haven't gotten over there yet."

Derick smiled. "Coney Island it is. Let's go."

When they arrived, Derick helped her out of the car and into the bright sunshine. "There's somewhere I want to show you," he said, as they started down the boardwalk.

He was mad at himself that he hadn't thought of bringing her here before. He led her off the boardwalk toward their destination. Her eyes widened when they approached.

"What is this place?"

"The Coney Art Walls," he explained. "The curators allow talented street artists to paint here. Awesome, right?"

Siobhan moved closer to inspect the painting in front of them—a colorful mermaid. "Yes, they're wonderful."

Derick couldn't help but feel pleased with himself. They wandered around hand in hand, looking at the eclectic variety of art. "Are any of these like the paintings you do?" he asked.

She hummed softly. "Some of them."

She didn't seem inclined to say more, too absorbed in the work in front of her, so he let her answer suffice.

They walked past each wall twice, and Derick had to admit, he'd never looked at paintings so thoroughly before he met Siobhan. But as Siobhan discussed the delicate line work of the Manhattan skyline, Derick could feel her passion as though she were physically transferring it to him. Her love for it was infectious and absolute.

It had been a long time since he'd been around love like that. It made him want to bottle up the experience and keep it with him forever.

But he'd have to settle for a different type of memento. "Come here," he said, as he put an arm around her waist and gently pulled her toward him, keeping their backs to a black-and-white painting that showed a lonely saxophone player in the subway. Derick pulled out his phone and held it in front of them.

"Are we taking a selfie?" Siobhan asked, and he could hear the smile in her voice.

He pinched her side, making her laugh. "Photography's art, too. Don't make fun of me."

She laughed and wrapped her arms around him. "Wouldn't dream of it."

Her words made him turn his head toward her as his finger snapped the picture. He kept his eyes on her until her gaze collided with his. He leaned in and pressed his lips to hers. It wasn't a passionate kiss like many of the others they'd shared, but it was no less meaningful.

They broke apart slowly, smiles appearing on both of their faces. "Let me see the picture," Siobhan said with a soft voice.

Derick brought the phone up, and they both looked down at it. Siobhan laughed again. "You're not even looking at the camera."

He shrugged. "Guess I found something more worthwhile to look at."

Siobhan's smile grew. "You're very smooth, you know that?"

Grabbing her hand in his, he led them toward the exit. "Yup."

She chuckled, and they walked back to the boardwalk, hands swinging gently between them.

They made their way down the boards, looking in shops and watching the tourists bustle by. As they walked past a young couple and their toddler, Siobhan remarked that the stuffed monkey the little girl was holding was cute.

Derick grinned at her as he walked toward the girl's father. "Excuse me. Where did you win your daughter that monkey?"

The father turned and pointed toward a water gun game that had a bunch of people milling around it.

"Thanks," Derick said, as he made his way toward the game, pulling Siobhan along behind him.

"I didn't say I wanted one," Siobhan said, laughing behind him.

"Well that's too bad, because I want to win you one." He pulled out his wallet and handed over his money before sitting down in one of the few open seats.

Siobhan settled her hands on his shoulders and leaned down to whisper in his ear. "Go get 'em, tiger."

Derick realized the anxiety he was feeling over a children's game was kind of ridiculous, but he didn't care. If Siobhan wanted a monkey, then he'd get her one, even if he had to stay here for the next hour and play this stupid game. Though he hoped it didn't come to that. He wasn't sure his ego could take it.

The buzzer sounded and the water began to squirt out of the hose. Derick aimed it carefully at the clown's mouth and said a silent prayer to whoever was the patron saint of games.

About thirty seconds later, the light above his clown began flashing. Before he could catch himself, Derick stood and thrust his fist into the air in victory. He looked around at his wide-eyed opponents—all of whom looked under the age of twelve—and slowly lowered his hand.

The game operator looked equally unimpressed. "Which will it be?"

Derick rubbed the back of his neck before pointing. "The monkey."

The guy handed it over, and Derick quickly presented it to Siobhan who smiled at him like he'd just solved world hunger.

Their shoulders bumped together as they continued their stroll down the boardwalk. Siobhan leaned toward him. "That was pretty hot."

Derick startled and looked over at Siobhan. "What was? Annihilating a bunch of kids for a stuffed animal?"

"No," Siobhan said with a laugh. She put her hand in the crook of his arm. "How badly you wanted to win it just because I liked it. *That* was what was hot."

Having no response, Derick pressed a chaste kiss to her cheek and kept walking.

When the sun began to set and the beach began to clear out, they decided to quickly grab two Nathan's hot dogs before making their way down to the beach to watch the sky change over the water as the sun descended.

They stood together, Siobhan's back to Derick's chest—his arms wrapped around her stomach—until the stars twinkled overhead.

"You know what else I've never done?" Siobhan asked.

"Hmm?"

"Swam in the ocean."

Derick turned her so she was facing him. "Never?"

Siobhan slowly shook her head. Her eyes were seductive, her smirk inviting.

"We should rectify that then," he said.

"We definitely should."

Suddenly, Siobhan sprang back from him. "Last one in loses an article of clothing for the walk back to the car."

And the race was on. Both of them quickly stripped down to their underwear and splashed into the ocean. Derick dove under waves and Siobhan tried to muscle through them. Derick got out to calmer seas first and waited for Siobhan.

"I win," he declared as she joined him.

"You did not. My foot hit water before yours did."

"But I made it out here first," he argued.

"I said first one in. Not first one *all* the way in."

Derick was quiet for a second. "I feel like I'm being conned."

He could just make out Siobhan's shrug in the moonlight. She wrapped her arms around his neck and her legs around his waist. "I'll make it up to you," she said, right before she pressed her lips to his.

She ground against him, and his cock got hard in an instant. His hands gripped her ass firmly as he pulled her tightly against his shaft.

A gasp left her lips as his erection pressed against her clit through her underwear. Their kisses were wild as they continued to grind together.

"Oh my God. Derick." Siobhan moaned as Derick's mouth ghosted down her neck.

"Shit, I'm going to come." Derick hadn't gotten off on rubbing against someone in years—maybe not since high school—but he'd be damned if he could think of anything sexier in that moment.

Siobhan's gasps of pleasure accompanied the gentle rolling of the waves. It was the most beautiful soundtrack Derick had ever heard.

They glided together a few more times before Siobhan began to quake in his arms with her release. He continued to rub against her, drawing out her orgasm as he kept pressure on the tiny bundle of nerves.

The water gliding over his sack, the soft friction against her underwear, and Siobhan's muffled pants of ecstasy all helped push him over the edge. He came in long spurts, his entire body bucking with the climax.

They stayed locked in an embrace for a few minutes before pulling apart slightly.

"I can't believe we did that," Siobhan said.

"Me neither. But I'm really glad we did."

They both laughed as they began the swim back to the beach. Once there, they waited a little while before getting dressed, allowing the warm night air to dry them slightly. When they finally reached for their clothes, Siobhan spoke.

"Hey, Derick."

Derick turned toward her as he pulled his shirt over his head. "Yeah?"

Siobhan smirked. "Lose the shirt."

Chapter 15

SIOBHAN PUT HER spoon down to rest on the small dessert in front of her. "The rest is yours," she said, pointing at the chocolate soufflé they'd been sharing.

"Really? You don't want anymore?" Derick asked. But he didn't wait for Siobhan to respond before finishing off the last few bites.

When the waiter returned to clear their plates, he said something to Derick in French, a language Siobhan had no idea Derick knew before tonight.

"What did he say?" Siobhan asked after the waiter had left.

"He said you're beautiful."

Siobhan looked at him in disbelief. "Seriously? He said that?"

Derick laughed and reached across the table to take Siobhan's hand. "No. He asked if he should bring the check. Guys don't tell other guys how hot their girlfriends are."

"Oh, right." Siobhan laughed softly.

"It's true though, you know. You are beautiful." Derick's

eyes warmed in the dim light of the elegant French restaurant, and Siobhan felt herself get lost in them.

"So," Derick said, "there's something I've been wondering, but I'm not sure how you'll feel about it."

"What?"

"I want to see your art." Derick looked eager, but she could hear the hesitation in his voice.

Siobhan was quiet at first. Her art was so personal to her. Sharing it with people always made her self-conscious. But there was a part of her that was excited to share her work with Derick. And the intimacy of it caused her to agree.

On the ride back to her apartment, Siobhan was a bundle of nerves. Not only would Derick be in the small space she called home, but he'd also see her paintings. It felt like a double whammy of judgment was waiting for her, and anxiety filled her.

They made their way into her apartment, and Siobhan turned on a few lights she had scattered around. Everything was visible from where Derick stood just inside the doorway. Her tiny galley kitchen, her bed, rickety table, overflowing closet that the faded pink dressing screen only partially obscured from view—it was all there like a beacon of economic hardship.

The only redeeming quality of the space—with its plastered ceiling and crumbling brick walls—was the floor-to-ceiling window that overlooked the bustling metropolis outside. To most it would just be a drafty window, but to a painter it was a dream—a frame that harnessed art that was in constant motion.

In an attempt to distract Derick from looking around her home, she walked to where she'd installed shelves on the far wall. "I put them here so the sun doesn't hit them."

Derick followed her over and spent a few minutes looking at the paintings. "It was smart to put them on shelves."

"Well, I don't have a ton of space, and I don't want them lying around where they could get messed up. You've seen how clumsy I am." Despite attempting to joke, her voice sounded small and unsure. She cleared her throat in the hopes of swallowing the feeling of inadequacy that swamped her.

"They're gorgeous."

His compliment warmed her slightly—made her shoulders relax. "Thanks."

"I wish I knew more about art." He never took his eyes off the paintings as he spoke. "I don't even know what style these are in?"

"Expressionism."

He finally tore his eyes away from her canvases and smiled at her. "I don't know what that is."

"The goal of expressionism is to show the emotional rather than the physical. To move beyond what our eyes can see and delve into what we feel. It tends to distort reality in order to affect the viewer's mood and ideas."

"Well, I'm definitely moved."

Siobhan smiled in response.

"Why did you choose this style?" he asked as he looked back at her paintings again.

"I saw Munch's *The Scream* when I was fourteen and that was it for me. The anxiety and alienation he conveys in that painting are…perfect. I looked at it and could imagine myself standing on that bridge, screaming for the world to both hear me *and* leave me alone." Siobhan shrugged the uncomfortable feelings away. "I was all in after that." She gave Derick a small smile.

He didn't return it, but rather looked at her in a way that she figured she probably looked at *The Scream:* a mix of awe and understanding. It seemed as though a spell was cast over them as he placed his hand on her cheek and drew her closer to him. And when their lips met, the spell exploded into a frenzy of hedonism that caused hands to grope, tongues to seek, and bodies to meld.

Siobhan barely registered her back hitting the mattress as Derick came down on top of her, his body heavy, but not overpowering as he held some of his weight off her with a forearm by her head. Her hands were in his hair, keeping his lips pressed to hers as he worked one hand under her red cotton summer dress.

His fingers skimmed along her flat stomach as goose bumps broke out from the tickling touch and the promise of where those fingers would eventually travel. He briefly drifted his hand up to caress her breasts over her bra before he trailed it back down her abdomen.

She bucked up into his touch, her lips parting from his on a gasp.

He took that opportunity to rain kisses along her jaw, nipping at her earlobe, and sucking on her neck. When his fingers found their way into her red lace thong, she instantly cursed herself for delaying this moment.

He rubbed her clit with the perfect amount of pressure to reduce her to a panting mess. By the time he leaned back slightly so he could thrust his fingers into her, she was making noises she hadn't even known she was capable of.

"Derick, I need you."

He brought his mouth to her ear and teasingly bit her lobe. "What do you need?"

"You. Inside me. Now."

He pushed himself up to standing and removed his wallet, extracting a condom from it. Then he yanked his pants and boxers down before sheathing himself and settling back over her. He brushed the back of his fingers over her cheek. "You're so beautiful." Then he leaned down and claimed her mouth in a sweet, yet all-consuming, kiss.

She felt his erection push at her entrance, and she wanted him there more than anything.

With both hands pressed into the mattress by her head, he finally thrust his cock into the tight heat of her body.

Their union was carnal and intense. She wanted this: for him to take her hard, to plunge deep, and to eliminate all distance between them. The way her legs brushed against his hips as he pistoned into her made her feel like the skin there could burst into flames.

He looked down at her intently. "I want to see you when you come. I want to watch you fall apart and know I did that."

His words were the sexiest things she'd ever heard. That, combined with the friction of his pelvis against her clit created a delicious encouragement toward the finish line.

Her orgasm continued to build, threatening to spill over with every sliver of contact.

His low groans of pleasure filled the room.

Another few thrusts were all it took to push her over the edge. She cried out with her climax as her body shook. He kept pumping into her a few more times before his movements stuttered and he came, filling the condom with his release.

They lay there for a while, catching their breaths and allowing the boneless feeling to pass. Eventually Derick got up and disposed of the condom.

With his body gone from hers, the warmth he'd created left, too. She glanced around her apartment and let the insecurities begin to creep back in. Pulling the blanket over herself, she stared at the ceiling and tried to calm down.

Derick returned and leaned across the bed so he was hovering over her. "Do I get to stay this time?"

Chapter 16

SIOBHAN AWOKE THE next morning nestled against Derick's strong body. With her eyes still closed, she lightly let her hand drift over his six-pack abs and toned pecs. *How was I considering telling him he couldn't stay last night?* She let her eyes drift open. *Oh, yeah.*

As her eyes adjusted to the light streaming into her dingy apartment, she tried to focus on the man in her bed. The man who was worth over a billion dollars. And not her shitty apartment.

"Why did you stop?"

She startled slightly. "What?"

"You stopped tracing me." He reached for her hand that had stilled on his chest and rubbed it up and down his torso. "It felt good. Do it again."

"I liked you better when you were sleeping," Siobhan replied as she let her hand caress him again.

He rolled over so he was facing her. "I like you all the time."

"Suck-up," she said, as she fought a smile.

He pressed his answering smile to hers. When he rested his head back on the pillow he studied her silently. Just as she was becoming unnerved by it, he spoke. "If I ask you something, will you tell me the truth?"

"Strike you as a liar, do I?" she teased.

"No, but you may not want to answer and I really want you to."

She lifted up onto an elbow so she could look down at him. "Okay. Shoot."

"Did you really want me to stay last night? Or did you just not want to turn me down again?"

Siobhan felt her eyes widen slightly. "What do you mean?"

"You're kind of hard to read sometimes, and I wasn't sure if you let me stay because you actually wanted me here or because I asked. Not to mention the fact that you fell asleep with your back to me." Derick said the words with a smile, but there was an earnestness to his expression that let her know he was invested in the answer.

Siobhan pushed a hand through his hair. "What happened to that clueless guy I met a few weeks ago?"

He smiled. "He's been paying more attention."

Siobhan flopped back onto the bed. "I don't know. I guess it's just that…it's weird…you're a billionaire and you're naked in my crappy apartment."

Derick quickly sat up and hovered over her. "Are you serious?" His tone and eyes weren't angry, just concerned.

She gazed back at him. "I know it's dumb. You never made

me feel insignificant or anything, and I've tried to do a really good job of forgetting how out of my league you are. But having you here"—she gestured around the room with her hand—"in my space. It was a lot to take in."

She tried to look away, but he held her chin between his thumb and index finger, not letting her escape. "First of all, I am *not* out of your league. You're stunning, and brilliant, and talented, and…Christ, Siobhan, you're dazzling. Everything about you amazes me. I'm just some schmuck who was lucky enough to keep you from falling on your ass."

She laughed, thankful that he'd restored some levity between them.

"Second of all, I didn't always have a ton of money, Siobhan. Growing up, we struggled. A lot. I don't want you to ever feel like we can't relate to each other." He leaned down and pressed his lips to hers.

She leaned up to kiss him again, thankful for the words, even though they couldn't be the truth.

Chapter 17

SIOBHAN RINSED THE remainder of the conditioner out of her hair until she could practically hear the strands squeak between her fingers.

She'd been hoping that her second shower of the day might rejuvenate her. Unfortunately, it hadn't. But she needed the second shower anyway. There was no way she was going out with Derick without one. Not after the afternoon she'd had.

A black lab puppy she was walking had decided a puddle looked like a good place to take a bath. She'd washed the dog before leaving the owner's apartment, which hadn't left her much time to get ready. Derick would be picking her up in less than a half hour to take her to a concert. It had been her idea to see this band, but now the thought of loud music and a late bedtime didn't sound nearly as appealing as it had originally.

Though she'd never admit it to Derick, Siobhan felt like she'd been burning the candle at both ends lately. She'd been doing her best to balance her hours at the Stone Room with painting, all of her other odd jobs, and seeing him, but it was proving difficult.

When she'd first moved to the city, she didn't have much of a social life. No real friends or boyfriend made it relatively easy for her to fit it all in. But now with Derick in her life—and she wanted him to stay there—she felt like he'd been fighting for whatever extra time she could spare. Though thankfully he hadn't mentioned it since their fight.

With no time to dry her hair, Siobhan sprayed something in it that would give her beachy waves as it air-dried. Then she applied some light makeup and put on a comfortable dress.

She answered her phone on the fourth ring after shuffling through her bag to look for it. "Hey, everything okay? I didn't think I'd talk to you until you got here."

"Yeah, sorry," Derick replied. "Everything's fine. I'm on my way and thought I'd see if you needed anything."

A nap. "No thanks. I'm good." She tried to suppress the yawn that snuck up on her as she spoke. "Or I will be once I find my other sandal."

"You sure you're okay?"

"Just tired. I'll get a second wind. Maybe a third if you're lucky." She did her best to make her voice sound light, but she could almost taste the staleness of the words as they left her lips.

"We don't have to go if you're not feeling up to it. We can do something else instead."

Siobhan wanted to protest, but since she had been the one

who suggested they see the band in the first place, she didn't think Derick would really mind if they canceled. "What did you have in mind?"

He was quiet for a moment and then spoke enthusiastically. "I'll go pick some food up at the store and make us dinner at my place. I'll have a car come get you in an hour and a half or so. It'll give you time to relax."

She'd never been to Derick's apartment, and the thought of a quiet dinner was too tempting to pass up. "Okay. That sounds perfect. I didn't know you cooked."

"Are you kidding? I love cooking."

Chapter 18

WHEN THE PENTHOUSE elevator opened directly into Derick's foyer, he was standing in front of it, waiting for her. When the doors opened to reveal a casual, yet stunning Siobhan, he couldn't help the smile that tugged at his lips. Nor the slight twitch of his cock.

"Thank you so much for this," she said, as she gave him a kiss hello. "I'm kind of burned out. A casual, relaxed dinner is...." Siobhan stopped speaking as she stepped past him and took in the room.

He looked around and tried to see it through her eyes. The thought made him cringe a little. The marble floors of his foyer gave way to dark hardwood floors that sat beneath his white furniture. The open space led out onto a large balcony where he had set up a candlelit dinner. *Candles were relaxing. Right?*

Siobhan walked in and scanned the space: his massive entertainment center, his floor-to-ceiling windows that overlooked Manhattan, the spiral staircase that led to the second floor. She looked overwhelmed.

"Wow, Derick. This is...this is really nice." She meant it. He could tell that much. But it didn't necessarily sound like she thought that was a good thing.

Derick didn't want the evening to get awkward so he stepped over to her and pulled her into a hug. "I missed you."

He felt her smile against his shoulder. "You just saw me two days ago."

"I miss you when you're not with me." The way she returned his hug and melted into him made him confident he'd made a positive turn in the evening.

"Excuse me, Monsieur Miller. Would you like to start the first course now?"

Derick felt Siobhan stiffen. "Yes, Philippe. That'd be great."

Philippe nodded and returned to the kitchen.

Siobhan pulled back slightly and looked over her shoulder toward the kitchen. "Who's that?"

"Philippe."

She rolled her eyes. "I figured that much. Is he, like, your own personal chef or something?"

"No, of course not."

Her shoulders seemed to sag in relief.

"He's a chef at Per Se."

Eyes widening, Siobhan took a step back. "You hired a chef from one of the most expensive French bistros in Manhattan. Even *I've* heard of that place."

Derick wasn't sure how to answer, so he just went with the truth. "Well, yeah. I guess."

She looked at him curiously.

Derick grabbed Siobhan's hand and pulled her out onto the balcony where he gave her a glass of champagne from the table. "I had a culinary emergency. So I called Arnaud, the owner of Per Se, and asked if I could hire one of his chefs for the night. We've done business together and become friends. It wasn't a big deal."

She looked out at the city skyline for a few moments before her gaze settled back on Derick's. Her anxiety was almost palpable. "Sorry, but I'm suddenly not feeling great. I think I need to go home." Siobhan walked over to a chair where she'd set down her purse and slung its strap over her shoulder. "I'll call you tomorrow."

Derick trailed after her as she began walking toward the elevator. "If you don't feel well, why don't you stay here tonight?"

"No, thanks. I have a bad headache. I wouldn't be very good company." Siobhan pressed the button for the elevator and the doors slid open. She turned to look at him.

"Siobhan—" Derick started, with a hint of anger and confusion in his voice, but Siobhan cut him off.

"'Night, Derick," she said, as she got on.

As the doors started to slide closed, Derick knew he was losing her. He darted forward and pushed the doors open. "You know, one of these times, you're going to run away, and I'm not going to run after you."

Chapter 19

SIOBHAN LOOKED DOWN at the elevator floor. "I can't do this, Derick."

"What is 'this' exactly?"

Siobhan raised her head, a humorless laugh leaving her as she lifted her hands at her sides. "It's everything. Penthouse elevators, private cars, a billionaire boyfriend. I can't do any of it. It's too much for me."

Derick's head tilted forward, showing the broad strength in his shoulders as he kept his arms braced against the elevator doors. "You can't or you won't?"

Siobhan shrugged. "Either. Both. Doesn't matter. It was never going to work. We should just end it now."

Derick straightened his posture and crossed his arms over his chest. She shouldn't have been thinking about how hot he looked standing like that, but she was. *Damn him and his muscles.*

"Tell me why."

Siobhan stood there silently, not knowing what to say.

"Don't I deserve an explanation?"

Hesitating for a moment, all Siobhan could do was nod her head and follow him off of the elevator when he stepped back.

Derick walked to the kitchen and leaned in. "Philippe, thank you for all you've done, but could we have some privacy?"

Philippe looked confused, and rightfully so. He hadn't even served them dinner and Derick was dismissing him. "Would you like me to at least clean up first?"

"I'll take care of it. Thank you."

Siobhan wandered into the living room while Derick showed Philippe out. When Derick returned, he settled onto his couch and looked at her expectantly.

Siobhan didn't know what to say or where to start. She looked at Derick, his amber eyes full of hurt. He was such a good man. A man who deserved the truth. "I know you went to a lot of trouble tonight, and I appreciate it. I do. But the hired chef, the formal dinner, I don't want any of that. I've already had it."

Derick leaned forward and rested his forearms on his thighs, looking confused. "What?"

"Look, I don't need to work tons of shitty jobs to make rent. I don't need to struggle to get by. I choose to live that way."

Derick looked confused. "Why?"

And there was the billion-dollar question. "I do it because I can't have the money *and* the art. I had to choose."

Derick's brow furrowed. "What do you mean you had to choose?"

Siobhan sighed and sat down in a chair across from him.

"My parents have money. Well, my stepdad does. Not billion-aire status, but he makes a good living. He and my mom run a successful cattle ranch in Oklahoma. They're hardworking people who can appreciate art as something you hang on a wall, or as a hobby at most. But they can't accept it as a full-time job. Especially not for their only child."

"So they refused to support you if you became an artist?"

"Basically"—Siobhan looked down at her hands—"yes. They helped me get through college, and I'm grateful for that. But I don't want their help anymore."

Derick stood and walked over to the balcony window, his hands in his pockets. He was quiet a minute before he turned back to her. "I don't get it. What does that have to do with me?"

"I'm feeling overwhelmed from every direction. I like you, really like you, but seeing you—well not actually seeing you, but being with you, reminds me of what could happen. My mother may have money now, but I didn't grow up that way. I'm uncomfortable with all of this.

"My mom married my stepdad when I was thirteen. My dad died in a car accident when I was four—I barely remem-ber him—but my mom was the best. She was a teacher, but her goal was to be a professor. She was taking night classes to get her Master's degree when she met my stepdad. And then…she just stopped."

"Stopped what?"

"Stopped everything. Stopped taking classes, stopped talk-ing about how much she loved teaching, stopped wanting to become a professor. When they got engaged, she quit teaching altogether. It was like her hopes and dreams completely collapsed and condensed to fit into his life, because *he* was the one with the money, so *he* was the only one who got a say."

Siobhan felt some of the tension leave with her words. But the cause for it was still there. "Your wealth is intimidating. Add it to the fact that I worry I'm reliving my mother's life, and I just…I'm scared, Derick. I'm scared that I'll just give up on my dreams because it's easier not to pursue them."

Derick's eyes narrowed. "You really think you'd do that?"

Siobhan sighed. "Not intentionally. But my mom didn't do it intentionally, either. No one knows how their life will turn out. Look at yours."

"That's true. But giving up on a dream is an active choice. A choice I don't think you'd make. Do you?"

Siobhan shrugged. "I don't know. College was a break from the easy lifestyle I'd become accustomed to, so I welcomed it. But I can't live like a college kid all my life, working a million odd jobs until my real career begins. Everyone has their breaking point. And I'd be lying if I said I want to live paycheck to paycheck for the rest of my life, chasing a dream I might never catch."

"You'll catch it." Derick's words came out so quickly she wondered if he actually believed them.

She swallowed hard. "It's just that looking at all of this"— she gestured around his apartment—"and doing all of these extravagant things with you, it just reminds me that I'll probably never earn a life like that on my own."

Derick breathed in deeply, and reached out to rub a calming hand on Siobhan's back. "You realize the majority of the world doesn't get to live a life like this, right?" Derick nearly laughed. "You can't compare yourself to me, because we aren't the same."

"Clearly." Siobhan laughed for the first time since she'd entered Derick's apartment. "Your bathroom's the size of my whole apartment."

Derick gave her a playful squeeze on the back of her neck, which made her shiver. "That's ridiculous. You haven't even seen my bathroom. It's probably only like half the size."

Then Derick pulled her in close and his voice sobered. "We're not the same because you have a goal you've been working the majority of your life to reach. And more importantly, you have the talent to actually achieve it."

Siobhan pulled back so she could look Derick in the eyes. "You really think that's enough?"

"I do." Derick gave her a kiss on her forehead. "Plus, you've got an amazingly sweet boyfriend who will do whatever it takes to cheer you up when you're upset."

Siobhan's eyes raked over Derick's hard body, which she just noticed looked especially delicious in his perfectly fitted dark-gray button-up. "Oh yeah? What did you have in mind?"

"Dinner?" he answered with an amused grin.

"Hmm, I was kind of thinking we could eat late tonight." Then she leaned in and pressed her lips to his.

Chapter 20

DERICK'S MOUTH MOVED slowly in response, parting hers with his soft tongue. Somehow it was exactly what she needed. All her remaining reservations seemed to melt away the moment she kissed him. Maybe that's why she did it.

Her body responded instantly as he leaned her back onto the couch slowly and held himself above her. His lips moved from her mouth down her jawline and neck and he stopped only to remove her shirt.

Neither of them spoke, and they didn't need to. The physical connection and the way their eyes locked as Derick slipped the rest of her clothing off said more than any words could have. She watched him undress, retrieving a condom from his wallet and sliding it over himself as he stood above her.

As he lowered himself to her, his skin pressing against hers, she ached to have him inside her. But it wasn't just a carnal need as it had been before. Their previous encounters had been full of passion—an urgent attack of hormones rushing them to an inevitable end.

This time it was something more—a slow melding of bodies as he pushed into her and the two of them became one, a slow rock of his hips as Derick moved inside of her. Their movements remained in sync as they gave each other gentle touches and slow kisses.

Gradually their breaths became heavier and their moans grew louder. What had begun as a steady climb was now becoming something else. It wasn't rushed or frantic or unpredictable. Just a quickening of Derick's thrusts and the smooth retraction as he pulled out almost completely before driving back in. It was warm, easy, comforting.

Siobhan felt herself get closer to release with every sharp jerk of Derick's hips, and she urged him on, wrapping her legs around him tightly to get the friction she craved.

She could see his muscles tensing, his neck flexing with the anticipation of the climax she knew they were both chasing. The noises escaping from Siobhan's lips became louder, more erratic. And Derick groaned softly.

Her nails clawed at his back as her fingers ran up his spine and back down to his firm ass. She couldn't hold off much longer.

Derick dropped his head to hers and let out a few soft curses against her ear. He told her how good it felt to be inside her, to have her to himself. And that was what did it. The tickle of his breath on her sensitive skin combined with the pull and push of his long cock had her tumbling over the edge, her body quivering below Derick's as he continued to drive deep.

As her orgasm began to subside, Derick found his own, his cock twitching sharply inside her as he let go. His hard thrusts became slow glides as he emptied himself.

Derick pulled back to look at her and ran a thumb along her jaw. "I have something I want to show you tomorrow."

Chapter 21

AFTER SLEEPING IN the next morning, Derick had a car pick them up. Other than saying he knew of a good diner that'd be a bit of a hike for them, he didn't tell her much about where they were going.

"I spy something blue," he said, once they got in the car.

Siobhan's head jerked toward his. "What?"

"I said," he replied, drawing out the words, "I spy something blue."

Her lips quirked up into a smile as her eyes scanned the car. "The driver's coat."

"You cheated."

A laugh burst out of Siobhan. "How can you cheat at I Spy?"

"I'm not sure, but you clearly managed it."

"Whatever. It's my turn."

Once the car came to a stop outside the city, Siobhan got out and asked, "Where are we exactly?"

"Forest Hills," he answered. Though he knew that didn't

mean much to her. She knew Brooklyn because she lived there, and was starting to become more familiar with Manhattan. But her knowledge of the other three boroughs was virtually nonexistent.

He looked down the tree-lined street in the quiet Queens neighborhood trying to remember what it looked like the last time he'd been here. It had probably been at least seven or eight years. But other than a few trees that had been removed from a yard across the street, the neighborhood didn't appear to have changed.

Derick thanked the driver and, after confirming with Siobhan that she didn't mind taking the train back to the city, he let him know that they wouldn't be needing him anymore today.

When the car pulled away, Derick put an arm around Siobhan, who looked in awe of the homes surrounding them. Derick couldn't blame her. He remembered what it was like to be amazed by homes like this. They were beautiful. Large, brick or stone colonials full of so much character and charm that even the landscaping told a story.

He threaded Siobhan's fingers through his and drew her hand up to his lips for a quick kiss and then brought it back down, giving a gentle squeeze. "I want to share some things about my childhood with you. I think it'll explain a lot about why I'm the way I am."

"Okay." She looked curious, though somewhat tentative.

"Starting with this house." Derick nodded toward the

three-story Tudor in front of them. Its plush green lawn was manicured to perfection, and the mature trees in the front yard cast shadows across the tan stucco in the late morning sun.

"Is this where you grew up?"

Derick gave her a small smile, one where his lips didn't even part. "No, I grew up in Queens, but not this part."

Siobhan tucked her wavy hair behind one of her ears, looking confused. "Then whose house is this?"

Derick breathed deeply, inhaling the scent of freshly cut grass. It was the one thing he couldn't get in Manhattan, no matter how much money he had. "I have no idea."

Siobhan's eyes narrowed.

"It's the house my mom always wanted. When my brother and I were growing up, she used to take us by here and tell us that one day she'd buy it for us. She loved the way the roofs were angled and how those flowers bloomed every year." He pointed to the bushes in front of the bay window. "She said we could make a treehouse in the backyard and that she'd plant a garden with tomatoes and peppers."

Siobhan looked up at him as he spoke, but she didn't say anything.

"It never happened though." Derick dropped his head and dug the toe of his shoe into a patch of grass in one of the cracks in the sidewalk. "We knew it wouldn't. Cole and me," he clarified. "At least, we knew once we got a little older. Some of these houses were close to a million dollars even back then. But my mom always said if she worked hard enough, eventually she could give us the home—and the life—we deserved."

"That's sweet. I think parents need to have dreams for their children. Even if those dreams never end up coming true."

"I guess so." Derick nodded slowly and looked back up at the house. "She passed it every day on her way to work after she got off the bus. Walked right down this street and by the house that would never become her home."

"Where did she work?" Siobhan asked.

"She cooked and cleaned for a family on the next block. The wife owned a boutique a few miles away, and the husband was a corporate lawyer in Manhattan. Had two boys right around our ages." Derick shook his head, imagining what her job must have been like. "It was like watching a life she knew she'd probably never get to have." Derick let go of Siobhan's hand and put his hands in the pockets of his navy-and-white plaid shorts.

"What about your dad?" Siobhan's voice was hesitant, like she wasn't sure whether she should be asking.

But he liked that she did. "My father never did a damn thing for us. Best thing he ever did was leave. I haven't seen him since I was three, and I don't want to." Derick rubbed a hand against the back of his neck. "My mom did everything on her own, and I never heard her complain. That's why I swore that one day I'd make enough money to buy her this house, take care of her like she tried to take care of us. I just didn't realize that when that day finally came, she wouldn't be here to enjoy it."

Derick looked down at Siobhan, whose eyes were tearing up. "When did you lose her?"

The question should have been simple, but it didn't feel that way. "Right after I graduated from college. Maybe a year or so before the app took off. The real kicker is that I probably could've knocked on the door and made them an offer they couldn't turn down, and that would've been it. But even if my mom had been alive at the time, she wouldn't have been able to live there on her own anyway. She'd been sick since she got diagnosed with ALS my sophomore year of high school. When she passed away, she was living with Cole and his wife upstate."

"I'm sorry."

"Thanks," he said, as they began walking up the street. "It's okay. Really. I've made my peace with it."

"So where *did* you grow up? You said it's around here somewhere, right?"

"In a place called Kew Gardens. It's a neighborhood nearby, but it couldn't be farther away from what we're looking at now."

"Are you going to show it to me?"

Derick shook his head. "Nah, there isn't much to show. Just a little two-bedroom apartment in a plain brick building. Why don't we get a bite to eat at the place I told you about instead, and then head back to the city?" Derick pointed up the street. "It's only like a ten-minute walk from here."

"Okay." Siobhan nodded and began walking with him. She was quiet for a few moments before she spoke again. "You could still do it, you know. Walk up to the house and make them that offer. It might make you feel better to have it."

Derick smiled. "Having things doesn't make me feel better. It never has." Their pace slowed until it stopped completely, and Derick turned to face her. "That's what I've been trying so hard to explain to you. It's doing things for the people I care about that makes me feel like there's some purpose to having all this money."

Siobhan was quiet for a moment, seemingly thinking about what she wanted to say. "I get where you're coming from. Really I do. But I can't be a way for you to make good on the things you wished you'd been able to do for your mom."

Derick sighed heavily. "I understand that. I know you want to make it without anyone's help, and like I told you before, I can respect that. But I can't unmake my money to make you happy, Siobhan. I brought you here to show you that I know what it's like to struggle.

"I have nothing to do with you feeling inferior. You're projecting those feelings onto yourself. So you're going to have to work with me on this." Derick looked back at the large house before turning to Siobhan again. "My mom used to say we were all just diamonds in the rough. We may not be shiny and beautiful in the moment, but with a little polishing, we could be the most dazzling things in the room. Not to mention the toughest."

Siobhan chewed on her bottom lip, her eyes watering.

Derick pulled her close. "I think the same thing could be said for you. But you need to believe in your own worth, Siobhan, and I'm willing to help you do that. Just tell me what I need to do."

Siobhan released a shaky breath, turning her head away briefly before turning back and looking into Derick's eyes. "I think"—she cleared her throat—"I think I need to get over it."

Derick couldn't resist the smile that spread across his face. "Are you serious right now?"

Siobhan returned his smile with a small one of her own. "Yeah. It's difficult, Derick. I can't lie about that. Being in a relationship where, in at least one sense, I can never be equal is tough for me. But not having you would be way harder. So I'll work on accepting that it's okay to let you help me sometimes."

Derick pulled her in for a firm hug. Planting a kiss on her neck, he buried his face in her neck.

She burrowed into him. "I'm sorry I drive you crazy."

Derick chuckled. "It's okay. I love you anyway."

Derick felt his heartbeat quicken, and he wondered if Siobhan felt it, too, as she pressed against his chest. He hadn't planned to tell her he loved her. At least not like that. But that didn't make it any less true.

Siobhan was silent, and Derick was scared of what might come out of her mouth when she finally spoke. So instead of waiting, he leaned down to capture her mouth with his. She didn't pull back or make any awkward movements that would indicate she was uncomfortable with what he'd said.

She just kissed him back, surrendering herself to him slowly on the quiet suburban street. He didn't need her to say she loved him, too. He didn't need her to say *anything*.

This was enough.

Chapter 22

"OH MY GOD! You're the worst." Cory's dark-brown eyes widened, and Siobhan felt slightly chastised by them. "He told you he loved you and you didn't say anything back?"

"In my defense, I didn't even have much time to formulate a response before his tongue was in my mouth."

Marnel sighed and let her head fall onto her palm as she leaned against the bar dreamily. "Tell us more about his tongue."

Siobhan laughed before heading back to the host's station. But she could feel the girls following, so she turned to face them. "Don't you have work you could be doing?"

Confusion swept across their faces. "We're waitresses and the bar doesn't open for a half hour," Cory answered. "Besides, we *are* working. Working on you not ruining your relationship. Again."

"Oh, stop. Not telling Derick that I loved him right after he said it isn't going to ruin our relationship." *Would it?* "We're not teenagers."

"And as far as the financial thing goes, we're on the same page now. I accept that Derick has money, and he accepts that he's not allowed to give me any." The girls knew about her previous fight with Derick, and they were supportive of her feelings. Even if they didn't completely agree with them. "I'll tell him how I feel eventually. I'm just waiting for the right time."

"Oh yeah? When might that be?" Cory asked.

Siobhan wished she knew.

Chapter 23

"SEVEN MINUTES."

Siobhan's head turned toward Kayla's voice. She hadn't even known the other artist had been standing nearby. "Really? You sure?"

"Yup." Kayla smiled warmly. "I think that's the longest anyone's stared at any of our paintings all night. How great would it be if one of us sold something?"

Siobhan felt her stomach squirm inside her body. "Pretty great." Her excitement was building at the prospect of someone purchasing one of her paintings. It seemed surreal. "I'm sure Andrew's already sold a few things. His section's been crowded since opening." She took a sip of champagne.

Kayla let out an exaggerated groan, but Siobhan could tell Kayla wasn't actually upset. Siobhan hadn't known either of the two other artists very long—only since they'd found out their work would all be displayed in the gallery on the same night. But they'd both seemed nice enough. And Kayla was way more relaxed than Siobhan when it came to making a name for herself. "I know. But he's been doing this for a while. He knows a lot of people in the city. It's so hard to make it in New York. That's why a lot of people have been moving to Detroit. Cheap rent, lots of exposure. I've considered it myself lately."

Siobhan pushed off of the counter she'd been leaning against and walked casually—she hoped—away from the bald-headed, middle-aged man who was still admiring one of her pieces. "Oh yeah?" she asked, taking another sip of champagne to calm her frayed nerves as the two moved toward Andrew's paintings, Kayla following close behind.

Just then she felt a pair of strong hands on her hips. "What did I miss?" Derick gave her a kiss on the cheek as he leaned in from behind her.

Siobhan looked around. "Bacon-wrapped shrimp and me hyperventilating. That would be the reason for this," she said, holding up the champagne glass.

Derick chuckled. "Damn. I love bacon-wrapped shrimp." Then he moved to stand in front of her, his hand taking Siobhan's and giving it a comforting squeeze.

She was glad that he'd come, but she was equally glad she'd told him to come closer to the end. She didn't want him seeing her freaking out the whole time.

"Derick, this is Kayla. She's one of the other artists whose work is being displayed tonight."

Derick extended his hand, and Kayla looked more than happy to take it.

"It's nice to meet you," he said. "And congratulations. You'll have to show me which paintings are yours."

Kayla smiled politely and thanked him. Then she excused herself, saying she had some things to attend to.

Siobhan walked Derick around the space, introducing him to Veronica, the gallery owner, and pointing out the other artists' work. He seemed genuinely interested, though Siobhan thought it probably had more to do with his excitement for her and less to do with his passion for art.

When they got to Siobhan's work, she didn't see the man who had been there earlier. There were a few others browsing leisurely, but none seemed exceptionally interested. And the crowd had started to thin somewhat.

Derick put a hand on the small of her back and handed her a new glass of champagne from the server's tray. Then he took one for himself. "I have a secret," Derick whispered as they stood in front of one of her paintings.

Siobhan gave him a curious sideways glance.

"I like your paintings the best." He said it softly, close enough to her ear that she could feel his breath as he spoke.

"Do you really? Or are you just saying that?" Siobhan was skeptical, but she hoped it was true.

"You think because I'm your boyfriend I'd just say I liked yours more than the others?"

Siobhan shrugged and gave him a smirk. "Maybe."

"I'm insulted. My preference for art is based solely on taste." Derick gestured with his free hand toward Andrew's section of the gallery. "And also on the fact that most of that guy's paintings look like giant dicks to me."

Siobhan nearly spit out the champagne she had in her mouth. "I'm not sure who that reveals more about, you or Andrew."

Derick laughed. "Good point."

Only a few people remained in the gallery, and as Derick and Siobhan circled back around one last time, Siobhan spotted the owner. "I'll be right back. I just want to thank her before we get going. Meet you outside?"

Derick nodded and headed for the door. As Siobhan walked across the hardwood floors toward Veronica, the nerves that had subsided slightly with Derick's arrival returned in full force. But she was able to keep her voice calm as she thanked the woman for the opportunity.

"My pleasure. And I'll certainly be in contact if anyone purchases anything. There were several people interested, but no sales just yet."

Siobhan couldn't help the disappointment that seemed to spread through her at the thought of no one purchasing anything. Even though she'd known the chances were slim, somehow she'd gotten her hopes up a little. She also felt a certain amount of pride knowing people appreciated her work, even if they didn't necessarily want it in their home.

On the way outside, Siobhan told herself that there was still a chance that someone could buy something. It was okay if no one did, that her artistic career would take time. But none of those things made her feel any better.

All she wanted now was to be alone. She wanted to put on comfortable pajamas and listen to loud music and binge-watch reality TV shows. She wanted to forget about not being able to prove to herself—and everyone else—that she could do this.

But as she exited the building into the evening air, which had gotten considerably cooler since opening, she looked at the man before her and all she wanted was him.

Chapter 24

AFTER THE ELEVATOR doors opened, Derick stood back while Siobhan entered. She'd been noticeably quiet on the way back to Derick's after the showing. He'd asked if she was okay, and she'd assured him that she was. But it was unconvincing. He knew her well enough by now that he could tell when something was bothering her.

Derick removed his hand from its place on Siobhan's lower back and headed toward the kitchen. "You want anything to drink?"

"Just water would be good." Siobhan followed him over and took a seat at the bar stool at his kitchen island, folding her arms on the dark granite countertop and exhaling heavily. She looked sad, and it didn't appear that she was trying to hide it.

After putting some ice water into a glass, Derick walked over to hand it to her.

"You sure you're okay?" Derick couldn't resist asking. He didn't care if she told him earlier that she was fine. She obviously wasn't.

She slid the drink between her hands but didn't take a sip yet. "Yeah. Nothing happened, anyway." She shook her head, and he could tell the small smile that momentarily grazed one corner of her mouth was forced. "The gallery owner said that there was some interest in some of my paintings, but I didn't sell anything during the show. I shouldn't even be upset. It's dumb."

"Why's that dumb?" Derick reached out to take Siobhan's fingers, which were rubbing the condensation off the outside of the glass.

Siobhan shrugged and let Derick take her hand in his. She was silent for a few moments as if she was thinking about his question. "I don't know. Because it's stupid for me to think that someone would want to buy something from an artist they've never heard of. And I didn't even really expect that someone would buy one. At least not yet. It doesn't make sense that I feel disappointed. But I am. I should just be happy that people got to see my work. That's the first step, right?"

"Yeah. But you can't help how you feel." Derick moved closer to her and spun the stool just enough so that she was facing him completely. He gave her a kiss on her forehead and clasped her other hand in his, rubbing his thumb over her smooth skin. "You'll sell something eventually." Though he believed it, he heard how generic it sounded. How unconvincing. But he had nothing better to offer.

"I know," she replied, her words rivaling his in their lack of conviction.

The two remained silent for a few moments before Derick's hands left hers to pull her into a hug. She leaned into him, her head resting on his chest as he stroked her hair.

Finally, she pulled back, breathing in deeply and raising her head to look at him. Her eyes seemed to hold a bit more hope than he'd seen in them earlier. "It's really fine," she said, though he wasn't sure if she was telling *him* that or herself. "I'm okay, just a little let down. I know this'll all take time. I have to get over the initial disappointment of it, I guess." Then she gave him a small smile, which seemed a bit more genuine than it had earlier.

He didn't like that he couldn't fix what was wrong. It didn't matter who he knew or how much money he had; this was something that was out of Derick's control. Siobhan would feel however she would feel. But right now he wanted her to feel good, even if that feeling wouldn't be permanent.

Bringing a hand up to her chin, Derick traced her bottom lip softly with his thumb for a moment before he brought his mouth to hers. It was a slow kiss, a gentle glide of their lips as Derick eased hers open with his own. It felt innocent at first, but as the moments passed, the soft touch of their tongues grew hungrier. Siobhan let out a low moan, her mouth so wet and warm he didn't think he could ever leave it.

As Siobhan's nails massaged his back through his shirt, Derick felt his cock twitch and then stiffen completely. He grabbed the sides of Siobhan's ass to pull her against him as he settled himself between her thighs. Then his hands were in her hair, on her breasts, sliding up her dress to feel the smooth flesh on her legs.

Finally he lifted her off the stool, her legs wrapping tightly around him as he carried her to his bedroom. Lowering her onto the mattress, his mouth moved to her neck and shoulders. Ever since he'd first seen her in her strapless black dress, he'd wanted his lips on her exposed skin.

As he lay beside her, Derick used one arm to support his weight, his other hand roaming Siobhan's body.

"Derick." Siobhan let out his name with a breath.

A soft sigh escaped Derick's lips in response. Every sound she made—every little whimper or word or low moan—made him even harder than he already was. He hooked a thumb in her lace thong and slid it down her legs and over her shoes. *The heels are staying on.*

Derick kicked off his own shoes and socks before beginning to remove his shirt. In the dim light from the hall, Derick could see Siobhan's eyes on him as he undressed slowly. He liked the way it made him feel—admired, wanted. He hoped that he made her feel the same way when they were together.

He ran a hand over the hard bulge inside his boxers and wiped the bead of moisture on the fabric.

She brought a hand to her stomach, and it continued its path slowly downward.

God, keep going.

Her free hand joined the silent caressing, drifting over the creamy skin of her breast as the other hand continued to drift down until it made contact with her clit.

There was an intimacy that turned Derick on more than anything else. He loved that she felt so comfortable with him.

Not able to watch her any longer without making physical contact, he was on her, his lips attacking hers and his fingers plunging deep inside her as she continued to stroke herself. He could feel how close she was as her body began to tense.

But he wanted to be right there with her when she let go. He wanted her clenching around him as he thrust into her slick warmth, chasing his own release. His cock ground against her thigh, and he knew he could come from that alone if he kept it up long enough.

But Siobhan took him in her warm palm moments later and turned to face him. She stroked his shaft, her fingers still slippery with her own desire. The softness of her hands combined with how tightly she was gripping him almost made him lose control. But he managed to hold off, trying to focus on her pleasure instead.

Moaning, she bucked against his hand and guided him so he was flat on his back. Then she did one of sexiest things he'd ever seen her do. She climbed on top of him, held his hands above his head, and rode the ever-loving fuck out of him.

He loved that she took control. It was something she hadn't done in the past, and it turned him on more than he'd expected. "Siobhan," he warned when he was dangerously close to coming. She was obviously aware that he didn't have a condom on. As was he. It had been so long since he'd felt this, he'd almost forgotten how incredible it felt, how perfect.

"Shh," she said quietly as she put a finger to his lips. "I want you to. It's okay."

And somehow Derick knew it was. So he allowed himself to thrust faster, his hands on Siobhan's hips, and her hair falling wildly over his chest as she finally lost control.

It wasn't long before Derick let go too, emptying himself inside her in long, sharp bursts.

The two lay there for a few minutes, Derick's hands around Siobhan until she finally climbed off of him and headed for the bathroom.

When she returned, she slid into bed beside him and rested her head on his chest. Her fingers skated over the hair there as she remained silent.

"Doing okay?" he asked, keeping his voice low so as not to upset the tranquillity of the moment.

She propped herself up on an elbow and looked down at him. "Still a little sad," she pouted.

Derick deflated. "Yeah?"

"Yeah," she sighed. "But I think if we do that at least two more times, I'll be good to go."

Derick took in the sparkle in her eye and the smirk on her lips. "I'll see what I can do."

Chapter 25

AS SOON AS Derick exited the Stone Room and walked out into the hotel lobby, he saw her. Siobhan was sitting on one of the couches, her legs crossed and her head propped against her hand as she leaned on the armrest. Blaine had said that Siobhan had come out to the lobby for her break. And from the looks of her, she needed it.

"Rough night?" he asked, as he took a seat beside her.

She barely looked in his direction before answering. "Something like that."

"Look," he said to her. "Whatever it is, it's going to be okay."

She gave a harsh laugh. "I wouldn't be so sure of that."

"I am." Then he reached an arm around her shoulder and pulled her into him. "You're done at eleven, right?"

"Yeah." She sighed. "Why?"

"I stopped by to see if you wanted to come over after your shift. But if you're tired, it's fine if you'd rather not."

"I am." She relaxed her head on his chest as he leaned back

against the couch. "But I have to get used to it because that's not going to change anytime soon."

"What do you mean?"

Siobhan's shoulders lifted into a small shrug. "It means that this is my life. And it'll probably *be* my life for the foreseeable future if I don't do something to change it. It's almost been a week since my art showing, and no one's bought anything."

"That doesn't mean they won't. You said yourself that it takes time."

"But how *much* time? Weeks? Months? Years? There's no way to know how long it'll take to sell even one painting, let alone make a career out of something that's a hobby to most people."

Derick hated how sad she sounded, how hopeless. "You're not 'most people.'"

"I'm not going to become some starving artist who's forty years old and living in the same shitty apartment because I can't afford anything better. And I'm not going to keep working a million different jobs to make ends meet." She shook her head slowly and pulled away from him. "I can't. Not when there are other ways to live."

"What do you mean, 'other ways to live'?"

"I mean right now it's not too late to figure out a different career path. I can still go back to school, get a normal job."

As hard as he tried, Derick couldn't picture Siobhan working some horrible nine-to-five office job or punching a time card somewhere. That wasn't the girl he fell in love with. "You won't be happy doing that."

Siobhan's weary eyes watered as she looked at him. "Maybe not." She shrugged again. "But I'm not really happy right now, either."

Well, shit. What the hell did that mean? Derick swallowed the lump in his throat.

"I'm sorry. I didn't mean us," Siobhan said, obviously sensing his fear. "It's everything else. The long hours, the guilt I feel for leaving my family to pursue a dream that may never become anything more than that. I don't know how much longer I can do it." She stood suddenly and smoothed her black skirt. "I have to get back. Saul's been on my ass lately, and I can't afford to lose the one job that's paying most of my bills right now."

"Okay," Derick said softly as he leaned in to give her a quick kiss. "Will you text me later and let me know about tonight?"

"Sure," she said, before turning around to head back inside the bar.

But Derick couldn't let her leave like that. "Do you know why Saul calls it the Stone Room?"

Siobhan's head whipped toward him, her body slowly following. "Because the walls are made of stone?"

Derick stood and walked toward her, shaking his head as he moved. "He said it was because he wanted to fill it with women who reminded him of rare and beautiful gems. The kind of girls everyone would want, but only a few would ever get to see up close."

He tucked a piece of hair behind her ear. "He may give you a hard time, but he sees how precious you are. I don't know how anyone could know you and *not* see it."

He saw a hint of a smile before she leaned up to press a kiss to his cheek. "Thank you for that."

"Anytime."

And as Siobhan returned to work, Derick wished he had more than words to give her.

Chapter 26

SIOBHAN LISTENED TO the phone ringing. "Pick up, Derick. Pick up, pick up," she chanted.

"Hey."

Siobhan could hear the smile in his voice—the warmness she knew he felt. "What took you so long?"

"To do what?" Derick sounded confused.

"Answer the phone."

"I'm confused. A phone only rings a few times before it goes to voice mail. How long could it have taken me?"

"Too long because I'm excited and want to tell you my great news!" Siobhan had started to bounce a little, her elation trying to find an outlet.

Derick laughed. "Okay, so tell me."

"I sold my paintings."

Derick didn't respond right away, causing Siobhan to deflate a little.

"Isn't that great news?"

"Of course! Yes, that's great news. I'm so happy for you."

"Thanks. I'm so thrilled. Veronica said they all went to the same buyer, probably the guy who'd been looking at them the night of the showing. She told me his name, but I was too busy screaming to hear her. I can't believe it." Siobhan felt emotion crawling up her throat. "I just…I needed this so badly, you know? Needed someone to like my work to prove that I wasn't wasting my time."

"I know, babe. And I'm so glad that you got the encouragement you needed." Derick cleared his throat. "We should celebrate tonight."

Siobhan smiled. "We definitely should."

Chapter 27

"SO WHAT'S THE plan for tonight?" Siobhan asked as she and Derick sat in the back of the Escalade.

"Well…promise you won't get mad."

Siobhan tilted her head. "I think that may be my *least* favorite answer to that question."

Derick shifted in his seat so that he was facing her. "I know how much you'd rather not do fancy things, but this is a special occasion. So can you just…not get freaked out?"

Derick looked so sincerely worried that Siobhan felt guilty for ever making him so concerned about how she'd react to his wealth. She reached over and threaded her fingers through his. "I can do that."

Derick seemed to sag with relief and smiled widely. "Good."

They rode in silence until the car stopped, and the driver opened the door. Siobhan held the hem of her red strapless dress against her legs as she got out. She turned to Derick. "The Met?"

Derick nodded.

"Is it open?"

Derick slid an arm around her waist and guided her toward the entrance. "For us, it is."

A woman met them at the door and said, "Right this way." Siobhan took in the opulence of the museum as they followed. Despite her telling Derick that she wouldn't freak out, Siobhan couldn't stop the memory of the Burger Joint popping into her head. She kind of felt like she had in that moment—a hoodlum surrounded by extravagance.

They ended up on the rooftop with gorgeous views of Central Park and the lights of the city seemingly in the distance. A single candlelit table set for dinner awaited them. Derick wrapped his hands around Siobhan from behind. "I know that I've already done the private-dinner-for-two thing, but it didn't go exactly as planned last time. So I thought we owed it another shot."

Siobhan leaned back into him and turned her head to face him. "I like the sound of that."

Their lips met for a brief kiss that managed to convey what words would never be able to: how far they'd come, how crazy they were about each other, how happy they made each other, how they'd be in it for the long haul.

Derick eased away and pulled out Siobhan's chair. A waitress came over immediately and began serving them.

They enjoyed the delicious meal of stuffed mushrooms and seafood risotto. The conversation flowed easily while they gazed at the beautiful view of Central Park until it got too dark to see much more than each other. When they finished, Derick checked his watch. "Perfect timing." He stood and held a hand out to her.

"For what?" Siobhan asked as she took his hand and allowed him to lead her to the edge of the roof.

Suddenly an explosion produced a giant rainbow of color in front of them.

Siobhan gasped. "Tell me you didn't get me fireworks."

She felt Derick vibrate with soft laughter. "Okay. I won't tell you."

"I can't believe it." Siobhan was mesmerized by the bright lights illuminating the sky above them.

Derick embraced her. "Is it too much?"

"Absolutely." Then she dragged her eyes away from the display and looked at Derick. "But I'm not going to lie. It's kind of cool to have a fireworks show just for me."

"You deserve so much more than that. But it's a good start," Derick said, before giving her a soft kiss on her cheek. He then turned back to the fireworks, and she did the same.

The finale was a brilliant explosion of color and sound. It was breathtaking.

When it was over, they faced each other again, and Derick spoke. "Down there," he gave a slight nod of his head toward Central Park, "when you gave me that art lesson, that was when I realized I'd found something that was going to become incredibly special to me."

Siobhan smirked. "A love of painting?"

Derick's lips twitched as he gave her a soft slap on her ass. "Don't ruin my moment."

"So sorry, sir."

Derick leaned forward so that his lips were almost touching hers. "I thought we talked about you calling me 'sir' that night at the Stone Room."

Siobhan pressed her breasts into his chest. "We did. But I was hoping that saying it might get me spanked again."

Derick gripped her ass with his hand. "Liked that, huh?"

Siobhan moaned softly and let out a breathless "Yes."

Derick kneaded the soft flesh under his hand. "Then I think it's time we left."

"Great idea. Your place is closer."

With that, Derick grabbed her hand and hurried back to the waiting car. They each sat against opposite doors on the drive back to Derick's apartment, staring at each other the entire way with a raw hunger that had Siobhan ready to come from eye contact alone.

Once they arrived at his building, they entered the elevator to the penthouse. As soon as the doors slid closed, Derick was on her. With his hands under her ass, he hoisted her up and thrust her against the mirrored wall. He devoured her mouth in a way that caused Siobhan to finally have to pull away and gasp for air.

Derick began nipping and sucking along her jaw and down her neck. He pressed his hard cock against her clit, only the fabric of his pants and her thong between them.

Siobhan tightened her leg around him and ground into him.

Derick moved his lips back up to her ear. "Tell me what you want me to do to you."

Siobhan moaned loudly. "Is there a camera in here?"

"No. This elevator is only for my use."

Siobhan pushed her hands through his hair and pulled his head away from hers. "Then I want you to make love to me in here."

"I can do that," Derick muttered. He let one of his hands slide from her ass, over her hip, and between her thighs. He gripped her thong and pulled, causing the material to rip off of her body. Her skin burned slightly when the silk pressed into her flesh before it gave way, but she welcomed the feeling. The pain only intensified the pleasure.

Siobhan left one hand tangled in Derick's hair as the other one drifted down his chest and stomach to his belt where she helped him undo his pants and push them to the floor.

Derick wasted no time thrusting into her, causing her spine to press into the glass with every push of his hips. It was exactly what she'd asked for, and she wasn't sure she'd ever let him have her any other way from then on.

The elevator was filled with gasps, moans, and cries of euphoria. Siobhan barely registered the doors sliding open on Derick's floor.

"Can you come like this?" Derick said through gritted teeth.

"Yes. Oh, Derick, yes."

His cock continued to plunge into her as the coarse hair on his pelvis rubbed against her clit.

"So good," he murmured against her neck. "You feel so good, Siobhan."

Siobhan pulled his hair again so she could attack his lips with hers. "Close," she mumbled as they kissed.

Derick pulled back slightly and gripped her ass harder. He pumped wildly.

"I'm going to bust, baby. I want you to come with me," Derick said.

Siobhan ground down hard, forcing her clit even tighter against him. "Oh, Derick, right there." She came with two more pumps of his hips, her entire body shuddering with her orgasm.

Derick followed, pushing his cock deep into her and holding it there as he released inside of her. He rocked against her a few more times, allowing her body to milk him fully.

As they came down from the high, both of them sagged into each other. Derick still held Siobhan, but their limbs were loose and exhausted. They peppered each other with light kisses on sweaty and sensitive skin.

Finally, they pulled apart enough to look at each other. Siobhan smiled. "We're going to celebrate like that every time I sell something."

Derick laughed. "Deal."

Chapter 28

SIOBHAN PULLED OPEN the door to Veronica's gallery and stepped inside. She slowed her gait, allowing herself to bask in the art that surrounded her. Just a week ago, her art had hung on these walls. And now she'd sold it. All of it. Siobhan had what it took to make it in the New York art scene.

"Siobhan, so nice to see you again." Veronica's voice pulled Siobhan from her musings. They did that weird air-cheek-kiss thing that seemed popular in New York.

"It's great to see you, too. I was excited to hear from you."

Veronica started walking, and Siobhan figured she was supposed to follow since Veronica kept talking. "Yes, it's a very exciting time. Especially to have sold all of your art to one buyer. You must have an admirer," Veronica said, as she shot Siobhan a sly smile.

Siobhan laughed. "My boyfriend probably wouldn't be too happy about that."

Veronica laughed. "You should play it up then. Keep him on his toes." They walked into the back storage room and over to where Siobhan's paintings were being held in preparation for shipment.

"You want to take one last look at them before we wrap them up?"

Siobhan nodded and slipped the covers off. She loved these paintings. She'd put her heart and soul into them. Hopefully their new owner would appreciate the love that had gone into every brushstroke.

Once she'd had her moment with the paintings, she helped Veronica wrap them.

"Can you hand me the address labels? They're on the shelf behind you," Veronica said.

"Sure," Siobhan replied as she turned to retrieve them. She looked down at the labels, curious as to where her benefactor lived.

Wait. It couldn't possibly be… "Are you sure these are the right labels?" Siobhan asked. She knew her voice sounded panicked, but she didn't care enough to act cool.

"Yes. Why?" Veronica narrowed her eyes in what was likely confusion.

"I can't…I don't." She gripped the labels tighter and looked at them again, begging them to magically change. He couldn't have done it. He *wouldn't* have. Would he?

But that was a stupid question. Because he clearly had. Roderick Miller was written on the labels she held. And his address matched Derick's. *Her* Derick. He'd been the one who bought all of her paintings.

Every ounce of joy she'd felt from selling her work evaporated as though she'd never felt it at all. She hadn't sold them because someone valued her work. She'd sold them because her boyfriend had felt bad for her.

But in a moment, her sorrow morphed into something more powerful. Anger. She didn't need to stick around with a man who treated her happiness as something he could buy—who treated her art as a pastime he would placate. Siobhan looked up at Veronica and in a steely voice, said, "Don't mail these."

"What? Why?" Veronica's voice sounded with disbelief.

"Because he doesn't deserve them."

Chapter 29

SIOBHAN STOOD INSIDE the ascending elevator, fuming. When the doors slid open, Derick was waiting for her. "This is a surprise," he said, happy to see her.

He smiled, but she didn't return it. "You want to talk about surprises? I've had a few of my own recently."

Derick's brow furrowed slightly. "You want to come in and talk?"

"No. I don't, actually. I think I can say what I need to from right here." She took a deep breath. "Besides, didn't you say that I shouldn't invite strangers into my apartment? I'm thinking I shouldn't get too comfortable in the apartments of strangers, either."

Derick's eyes narrowed in what seemed to be confusion. "What are you talking about, Siobhan?"

"You didn't even trust me enough to tell me your real name."

Derick opened his mouth, but then shut it.

Siobhan rolled her eyes. Even he knew there was no way to explain himself.

"Is that what this is really about? My name?" Derick asked.

Siobhan looked away and let out a disgusted laugh.

Derick reached out hesitantly toward her hand, but she crossed her arms over her chest before he could make any physical contact with her.

"No. It's not about your name. It's about the fact that you're the one who bought all my paintings. I guess you didn't think it was important enough to tell me that, either."

Derick didn't know how to respond.

"Congratulations. You managed to find another way to make me feel like a complete failure."

Derick's faced softened. "I didn't do it to make you feel like a failure. I did it—"

"Save it, Derick. Or Roderick. Or whatever the hell your name is."

"Siobhan, please. Just listen."

"There isn't anything you can say that'll excuse what you did," she said. "And do you really think you should dig yourself into an even bigger hole right now?"

She could tell from the way Derick's mouth parted that he wanted to say something. Thankfully he didn't. She needed him to hear her final words to him so she could let him go.

"After everything we've talked about, everything I've told you about my issues with your money and about how important my art is to me, I really can't believe you'd do something like this." Tensing her jaw, Siobhan pressed her lips together roughly. "I thought you supported me. It's bad enough my parents—"

"I did support you. I *do*. That's why I bought them. To help you."

"Don't do that." Her voice had a cold, hard edge to it. "This doesn't help me. And you knew that, or you wouldn't have kept the truth from me."

Siobhan kept her spine erect. "You took me out to celebrate, Derick." With her arms still crossed, she narrowed her eyes at him. "You let me be proud of an accomplishment I didn't achieve. Do you have any idea how that feels?"

Derick shook his head, his chin to his chest and his hand wringing his brow.

"Of course you don't. If you knew, you wouldn't have bought my paintings." She took a step back from him. "I'm done with this. All of it."

With that, Siobhan squared her shoulders and pressed the button for the elevator to return to the lobby. She was leaving everything behind that didn't support her: her high-handed boyfriend, this exhausting city, a job that valued her appearance over anything else. If Siobhan was going to find herself, it would have to be in a place with a community that would build her up as an artist instead of tear her down. A place like the one Kayla had suggested.

That settles it, Siobhan thought. She was going to move far, far away. And nothing was going to hold her back.

HE'S WORTH MILLIONS, BUT HE'S WORTHLESS WITHOUT HER.

After a traumatic breakup with her billionaire boyfriend Derick, Siobhan moves to Detroit, where she can build her painting career on her own terms. But Derick wants her back. And though Siobhan's body comes alive at his touch, she doesn't know if she can trust him again....

Read on for a sneak peek at the steamy second book in the Diamond Trilogy, *Radiant,* available only from

HEFTING HER BAG higher onto her shoulder, Siobhan waited for the light to turn green so she could cross the busy intersection. As she transferred her weight from one foot to the other, Siobhan's impatience escalated. She needed to paint.

The phone call from the girls the previous night had kick-started an emotional storm of Dust Bowl proportions. Every thought was hidden beneath a thin film of all things Derick.

As she continued walking toward her studio, Siobhan cursed Marnel for approximately the five hundredth time. She had worked so hard to actively *not* think of Derick over the past month, and it had been working. Perhaps she hadn't been completely happy yet, but she'd been getting there. Making new friends, finding a well-paying job, and having her art be well received had all been major stepping-stones toward an improved mood for Siobhan.

But now she was grumpy. And tense. And…sad. *Damn Marnel.*

Siobhan turned her head to look into her favorite coffee shop. Since she'd barely slept the night before, a caffeine boost would come in handy. But as she gazed in the window, her heart nearly leapt out of her chest. She jerked to a stop, not because of what she saw *through* the window, but because of what she saw reflected *in* it. Or *who,* rather.

Her sudden stop had caused a man to barrel into her, breaking her focus.

"Sorry," they both muttered as the man proceeded down the sidewalk, and Siobhan's eyes darted back to the window.

He was gone. But she was sure she'd seen…no it couldn't have been. She hadn't heard from him since she'd left New York. Siobhan shook her head. Now she wasn't just thinking about him, but she was imagining seeing him, too.

Tightening her grip on her bag, she quickened her pace toward her studio where she could lose herself in her work and forget all about him.

As if it'd be possible to ever forget Derick Miller.

About the Author

ELIZABETH HAYLEY is actually "Elizabeth" and "Hayley," two friends who love reading romance novels to obsessive levels. This mutual love prompted them to put their English degrees to good use by penning their own romances.

HER SECOND CHANCE AT LOVE MIGHT BE TOO GOOD TO BE TRUE....

When Chelsea O'Kane escapes to her family's inn in Maine, all she's got are fresh bruises, a gun in her lap, and a desire to start anew. That's when she runs into her old flame, Jeremy Holland. As he helps her fix up the inn, they rediscover what they once loved about each other.

Until it seems too good to last…

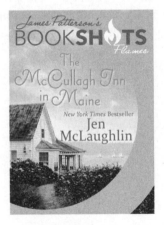

Read the stirring story of hope and redemption,
***The McCullagh Inn in Maine,* available now from**

THE GOLDEN BOY OF FOOTBALL JUST WENT *BAD*.

Quarterback Grayson Knight has a squeaky-clean reputation—
except when he's suddenly arrested for drug possession. Even
though she's on the opposing side of the courtroom, DA's
assistant Melissa St. James wants desperately to help him—and he
desperately wants her....

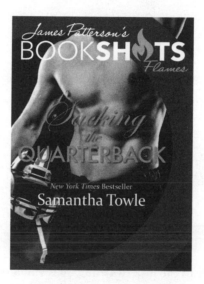

**Read about their thrilling affair in *Sacking the Quarterback*,
available now from**

SHE NEVER EXPECTED TO FALL IN LOVE WITH A COWBOY....

Rodeo king Tanner Callen isn't looking to be tied down anytime soon. When he sees Madeline Harper at a local honky-tonk—even though everything about her screams New York City—he brings out every trick in his playbook to take her home.

But soon he learns that he doesn't just want her for a night.

Instead, he hopes for forever.

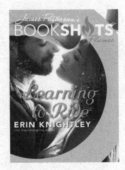

Read the heartwarming new romance, *Learning to Ride,* **available now from**

"I'M NOT ON TRIAL. SAN FRANCISCO IS."

Drug cartel boss the Kingfisher has a reputation for being violent and merciless. And after he's finally caught, he's set to stand trial for his vicious crimes—until he begins unleashing chaos and terror upon the lawyers, jurors, and police associated with the case. The city is paralyzed, and Detective Lindsay Boxer is caught in the eye of the storm.

Will the Women's Murder Club make it out alive—or will a sudden courtroom snare ensure their last breaths?

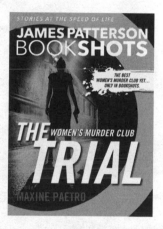

Read the shocking new Women's Murder Club story, available now only from

BOOK**SHOTS**

"ALEX CROSS, I'M COMING FOR YOU...."

Gary Soneji, the killer from *Along Came a Spider,* has been dead for more than ten years—but Cross swears he saw Soneji gun down his partner. Is Cross's worst enemy back from the grave?

Nothing will prepare you for the wicked truth.

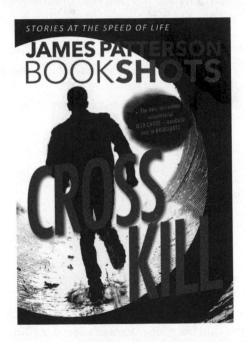

Read the next riveting, pulse-racing Alex Cross adventure, available now only from

BOOKSHOTS